THE GUNSMITH

#8

QUANAH'S REVENGE

Other Books
By
J.R. Roberts

Macklin's Women
The Chinese Gunmen
The Woman Hunt
The Guns of Abilene
Three Guns for Glory
Leadtown
The Longhorn War
Quanah's Revenge
Heavyweight Gun
New Orleans Fire

THE GUNSMITH

#8

QUANAH'S REVENGE

J.R. ROBERTS

SPEAKING VOLUMES, LLC

NAPLES, FLORIDA

2012

THE GUNSMITH

#8 QUANAH'S REVENGE

ISBN 978-1-61232-611-5

Dedication

To: Joe Lansdale, Bill Fieldhouse, James Reasoner, Steve Mertz because we're all in the same boat.

Historical Note

In the year 1836, nine-year-old Cynthia Ann Parker was taken captive from Parker's Fort, in Texas, a stockaded cluster of homesteads set up by her parents near the town of Grosebeck, Texas. Cynthia Ann was one of five white women and children abducted by the Comanches during a raid. The Comanches suffered from a low birthrate and Cynthia Ann readily adjusted to Indian life and was adopted. In her teens she became the wife of Peta Nacona, a rising young chief of a band of Comanches called Noconas. Early in the marriage she gave birth to a son and named him Quanah. Quanah looked like any other full-blooded Comanche infant, except that he had blue/gray eyes, instead of black. Twenty-four years later, forty Texas Rangers and twenty-one U.S. Cavalrymen struck a band of Noconas camped near the Pease River, killing a number of them and taking captives. After the battle they noticed that one of the women had Caucasian features and blue eyes. Her identity was suspected and Cynthia Ann's uncle was called for and identified her. They took her and her daughter, Prairie Flower, back to East Texas to live with the Parkers. Her relatives meant well, but Cynthia Ann attempted to escape several times, and in 1864, after her daughter died of a disease, she starved herself to death.

Not only did Quanah lose his mother and sister, but his father also died, and so did his brother, Pecos. After that, Quanah left the Noconas and joined the Kwahadies Comanches. He was probably attracted to this particular band of Comanches by their reputation as persistent and skillful raiders. In the late 1860s, Quanah—later to be called Quanah Parker by the whites —became the last great Comanche chief.

While the tribe's other war leaders were marching their defeated bands to the Fort Sill reservation in Indian Territory, Quanah and his Kwahadi band continued their murderous attacks on frontier settlements across half of Texas. In 1870 a crack army colonel named Ronald Slidell Mackenzie, was brought in to put a halt to the raiding in Texas.

Prologue

The Staked Plains
West Texas - June, 1873

"When is this fucking savage supposed to show, Jed?"
Amos Holt asked, mopping his face and neck with his
bandanna.

"Don't let him hear you say that, Amos," Jedediah
Jordan told his partner. "This is no ordinary savage."

"Yeah, yeah, I know, I heard all the stories about the
big Comanche chief, Quanah Parker. Big deal, he's just
a redskin. You'd think he was God, or something."

"He is a god," Jordan said, "to his people. They'd
follow him right to hell, Amos. Right straight to hell,
where we'll probably meet them, sooner or later."

"Can't be later enough for me," Holt said, staring up
at the hot sun that was baking his skin. "Fucking sun,"
he muttered, mopping the newly formed sweat from his
brow.

"Yeah," Jordan said.

He searched the plains with keen eyes, looking for
some sign of life. The two men were sitting in the shade
of their Conestoga wagon, seemingly out in the middle
of nowhere—only this wasn't nowhere. This was the
Staked Plains, where Quanah Parker and his Kwahadi
Comanches returned after their killing raids. Things had
been quiet of late, because 124 Comanches had been

1

taken captive by Colonel Ronald Slidell Mackenzie and his soldiers. Mackenzie, whom General Ulysses S. Grant himself called "the most promising young officer in the army," had been called upon in 1870 to use his expertise in stopping Quanah Parker and his braves, and the two had been butting heads ever since.

Although the captured Comanches were of the Kotsotekas tribe, their capture was a blow to the morale of all Comanches, Quanah Parker's Kwahadies included. They suspended their raiding for some time, and the U.S. government interpreted this to mean that they were prepared to join the bulk of the Comanche nation, which had accepted "peace" and was living on a reservation at Fort Sills, in central Texas. As a show of faith, the government released the captured Indians. They had no way of knowing that the Comanche raids were suspended only because Quanah feared cruel reprisals against his captured brothers and sisters. Now that they had been released, there was nothing to keep Quanah Parker from resuming his murderous revenge against the whites. And Quanah's actions were in part to avenge the deaths of his mother and sister.

Jordan was here to do business with Quanah Parker, to sell him the weapons he needed to resume his raids on an even larger scale than before. The fact that these weapons would kill many of his own kind did not concern Jed in the least. The only thing that concerned him was the money he would make selling the stolen cattle with which Quanah would pay him for what was in the wagon.

Ten cartons—twenty to the carton—of the new Winchester 73. Two hundred of the most accurate, reliable rifles ever manufactured.

"Shit, come on, you lousy redskin sonfabitch," Amos Holt said savagely.

Holt and Jordan had been partners for some time in all kinds of illegal dealings, with Indian as well as white, but this was the biggest deal they had ever been involved with—and this was just the start. Jordan knew he could get rich off of this deal.

"Stay calm, Amos," he said to his partner. "If these Comanches even smell fear on you, you've had it."

"Shit, Jed, I never had to come with you before. Why now, all of a sudden?" Holt asked.

"Because this is the biggest deal of our lives, Amos. Quanah wouldn't deal unless he saw both of us. These 'savages' have a high sense of honor, and they won't deal with anyone who won't confront them face to face."

"Why did you have to tell them about me?" his partner whined.

"What?" Jordan asked. "Would you want me to lie to Quanah?"

Holt let the air out of his lungs in a long, disgusted sigh and mopped his face again.

Jed Jordan was a man of nearly forty years, tall and gangly, and a very able man with his fists and his guns. His face bore the marks of many fights; few of them had been lost, and even those were eventually avenged. Jordan was a hard man and when something was worth taking, he took it, one way or another.

Amos Holt, on the other hand, was Jordan's opposite in every way, save one. He was just as greedy and just as willing to use whatever methods necessary to satisfy his greed. He was a man of medium height, grossly overweight and extremely soft—and very pale, which was the reason he hated the sun so much. Even a few moment's exposure could cause his skin to break out in splotches and then blisters.

Amos Holt's greed was surpassed only by his cowardice. He joined forces with others who were strong enough to help him satisfy his avarice, which explained his partnership with Jordan, a man ten years younger than he, braver and more vigorous and also—unknown to him—even greedier.

"There," Jordan said suddenly, and Holt looked up quickly.

"Where?" he asked, sounding panicky.

"There," Jordan said, again, but this time he pointed.

He saw them. There were only about ten or fifteen of them and as they approached closer and closer he could see the man leading them. He sat tall on his pony, with broad shoulders and a deep chest.

"Sit still," Jordan hissed as Holt began to fidget.

"Shit," Holt whispered, "that's him, ain't it?"

"That's Quanah," Jordan said. "Don't move until I do, all right? And for God's sake, don't say anything. They see you sweating, they'll think it's the sun, but if they hear you talk, they're gonna know you're scared shitless. I don't want to die just because you're a coward. Understand?"

"Y-yeah, yeah, I understand."

"Okay, then shut up."

As Quanah Parker and his braves closed the distance between them and the two white men, Holt could see that the Comanche chief wore a sidearm, which, from what he'd heard, was unusual. He had never seen a Comanche this close before, and he wished he wasn't seeing this one now.

The Indians came to within twenty feet of Holt and Jordan and then stopped. The powerfully built chief easily dismounted and approached the white men on foot. Quanah Parker did not look anything like what Holt expected an Indian to look like. The most striking thing about the man was the fact that he had blue eyes. Indians weren't supposed to have blue eyes, were they?

"You have my weapons?" the chief asked Jordan. He

ignored Holt, for which the fat man was very grateful. He was afraid that if the Indian looked directly at him, he might puke.

"In the wagon. Have you paid my price?" Jordan asked.

Quanah reached behind him and produced a large bowie knife with a bone handle, and Holt's stomach churned. He fully expected to see the big Indian plunge the blade into his partner's stomach, but instead the chief handed it to Jordan, handle first.

Holt didn't know it, but that was the sign. When Quanah's braves had delivered the cattle to a designated point, one of Jordan's men had given one of the braves the knife, which was Jordan's, as proof of payment. Jordan knew that the Indians couldn't have killed his men and found the knife, because he'd instructed his man, Cates, to hide the knife and not produce it unless the price had been paid. By that time, the rest of the men with Cates would have had time to become on guard. Of course, this was all just a precautionary measure. Quanah had never doublecrossed Jordan before, and he hadn't expected that he would this time, either.

Jordan accepted the knife and returned it to his belt, where it belonged.

"The price has been paid," the Comanche chief said.

"The rifles are in the wagon," Jordan said.

Quanah made a motion and some of his men dismounted to empty the wagon. They set about removing the cartons and loading them on the extra ponies they had brought with them.

When they were all loaded, Quanah turned to Jordan and said, "You will have more, soon?"

"I will have more," Jordan assured him.

Quanah nodded and prepared to return to his pony.

"I have a favor to ask," Jordan said, loud enough for Quanah to hear, but too soft for Holt to have heard.

Quanah turned and gave Jordan an impassive stare.
"An arrow," Jordan said.

Quanah continued to stare, then motioned to a brave
behind him, who stepped forward, took an arrow from
his quiver, and handed it to Jordan.

"Thank you," Jordan said to Quanah.

Quanah didn't reply, he just turned, walked back to
his coal black pony, mounted up and led his men away,
carrying 200 Winchester 73 rifles.

Jordan turned around and walked back to the wagon
and to Holt, who was sweating even more than before,
and not just from the sun.

"Scared?" Jordan asked Holt.

"Shit," Holt said in disgust.

"You were scared, weren't you?" Jordan asked.

"Hell, yeah, I was scared," Holt replied. "So what?"

"Amos, I think I can fix it so that you'll never be
scared again," Jordan told his partner.

"Shit," Holt said again. He didn't like being made fun
of. He knew he wasn't a brave man, but so what? Most
of the brave men he ever knew were on boot hill, and he
was still walking around.

"What's that for?" he asked Jordan, indicating the
arrow.

"This?" Jordan asked, holding the arrow out, point
towards Holt. "This is a souvenir."

"Souvenir?" Holt asked. "What the fuck you want
with a souvenir?"

"Oh, it ain't for me, Amos," Jordan told him, "it's for
you."

"Wha—" Holt started, but his words turned into a
scream as Jordan thrust the arrow forward with all of
his strength. The arrow cut through the fleshy folds of
Amos Holt's belly. His eyes popped wide open and so
did his mouth. His fat hands clutched at the arrow,
wanting to pull it out, but there was no strength in them.

Jed Jordan watched as his partner—his former partner —sank to his knees, still trying to grab the arrow hard enough to pull it free.

"Here, Amos, let me help you."

He reached down with both of his hands, grabbed the feathered shaft and pushed it in even further.

Amos Holt made a strangled noise in his throat and fell over onto his back. The sun, which he hated so much, beat down mercilessly, baking his skin, burning his eyes, but he hadn't the strength to shield his eyes, or to turn his head. He would lie there, staring up into that hot yellow ball of fire, until he bled to death.

Which would take a very long time.

Chapter One

Fort Sills, Texas - 1873

June was going out hot, and July was coming in hotter. If I could have bypassed Fort Sills, I would have, but I was out of water, and one of my team was coming up gimpy. If I walked him any further, I didn't know how much damage would be done to his hoof, so I wanted to have him checked.

The hardbaked ground immediately outside the fort was literally littered with Comanche braves, old men, women and children. These were the Comanches who had surrendered, signed a peace treaty, and agreed to live on the Fort Sills reservation, until room could be made for them to live elsewhere, permanently.

Guiding my team through the sea of people, I could see that most of them looked half-starved or sick; some looked half-dead. Teepees had been erected for them to live in, but there were so many of them assigned to one teepee that many of them were forced to lie around outside of them.

About twenty yards from the front gates of the fort my attention was attracted by a commotion near one of the teepees. A young Indian girl was screaming, apparently being chased by three soldiers.

I pulled my rig to a stop and watched for a few moments. They chased her around for a while and couldn't catch her until they split up and surrounded her. She was screaming, they were laughing, and by the time they grabbed her, I was moving.

Two of them were pinning her to the ground and the third one had ripped the top of her buckskin dress down to reveal her young breasts. They were underdeveloped breasts, barely more than two small lumps on her chest. She could scarcely have been more than twelve or thirteen years old, but what the three soldiers had in mind was obvious.

She was still screaming and the three men were still laughing when I reached them; they wouldn't have heard me if I'd simply chosen to tell them to let her go, so I didn't speak, I acted.

I grabbed the third man, who was struggling to get on top of her, by the shoulders and pulled him off. I yanked him hard enough to send him staggering back a half-dozen feet to fall on the ground.

The other two men were on their knees, each holding one of her arms. When they saw what I'd done to their friend they began to rise. I kicked the one on my left in the chest, sending him sprawling, and I backhanded the one on my right, also knocking him down. Then I reached down for the girl and hauled her to her feet.

"Get out of here," I told her. I didn't know if she understood me, but she took off like a scalded jack rabbit.

"Mister," a voice behind me said, "you just made a big mistake."

I turned to face the first man I'd thrown to the ground. He was a stocky man of about thirty-five, and on his arms were three stripes.

"Sergeant," I said, as he faced me with his arms dangling at his sides, "if you or any of your friends goes for their guns, you're going to be the first one I kill."

His eyes flicked down to my gun, and then back up to my face.

"I'm not going to take a beating, either," I warned him. "I'll blow the kneecap off the first man who tries it. Now you tell me, is a twelve-year-old Indian girl worth a kneecap—or your life?"

I had maneuvered myself so that I could keep all three of them in sight. The other two had picked themselves up off the ground and were standing on my other side. They were younger than the sergeant, and they had two stripes on each arm. They were looking to him for guidance, and he was looking at me, trying to decide if I really meant what I said.

He had no trouble making that decision; he could see the answer in my face.

"Shit, no," he said, finally. "No squaw is worth that," he told his friends, and then he directed his attention back to me and said, "But you ain't heard the last of this, mister. You count on that."

"I will," I replied. "I surely will. Now why don't you boys just mosey on back to wherever it is you're supposed to be."

The sergeant starting moving away, and the two corporals followed, but before they got out of earshot the sergeant told me one more time that I wouldn't hear the last of this, no way, no how.

I had as good a look at his face as he had at mine, and I knew that he was telling the truth, too.

Chapter Two

When they opened the gates to allow me into the compound, I asked where I could find a blacksmith and a saloon. I was instructed to drive my team all the way through the compound to the section of the fort that was a town. Go left and find the livery, go right and find the saloon. Take your choice which one you want first.

What I wanted first was the livery. I wanted the guy to tell me to go to the saloon and have a few drinks, and that my team would be ready to roll when I came back.

"Looks like he picked up a stone bruise," the liveryman told me.

"When can I leave?" I asked him.

"I'd say stay overnight and give him a chance to rest. I'll take another look at it in the morning. If he walks on it, it's only going to get worse."

"How far to the next town?"

"Too far."

"Okay, take care of him—and extra care of my black, okay?"

"You can count on it," he said. He was about my age, and he appreciated good horse flesh. I felt sure he'd do right by Duke. He didn't gush over the big horse like most people, but I could see the appraising look he was giving him. I wasn't worried about any of my animals when I left there.

I went back the other way and found the saloon. The town behind Fort Sills was hardly two streets long, and behind those two streets there were scattered houses where businessmen and some soldiers' families lived. It was hardly what you would call a thriving community.

The saloon was not only a saloon, it was a trading post and a general store, all rolled into one. There were a few wooden tables, and I ordered a beer and sat at one of the tables to nurse it.

As it turned out, I didn't have time to.

Four soldiers came walking into the place, and I recognized one of them: my friend, the sergeant. He hadn't wasted any time seeing to it that I didn't hear the end of the incident.

They approached my table and the sergeant said very politely, "Excuse me, sir. What is your name?"

"Clint Adams," I answered.

"Mr. Adams, we would like you to accompany us, please," he said.

"Where?" I asked.

"Please, sir."

"Not until you tell me where," I said.

He compressed his lips in annoyance. "Mr. Adams, our commanding officer would like to see you. If you do not choose to accompany us, we will be forced to place you under arrest."

"In that case," I said, "why not? I'm sure he'll want to hear how three soldiers tried to rape a twelve-year-old Indian girl." I got up. "Let's go, sergeant. I'm actually eager to meet your commanding officer."

Chapter Three

The sergeant and his two privates marched me from the saloon and through the compound. None of them spoke to me while we walked, and I likewise made no attempt to speak with them. I wondered what kind of a defense the sergeant was going to put up against my charge of attempted rape on that little Indian girl.

We entered an anteroom where a master sergeant sat at a desk; *my* sergeant left me by the door and went over to talk to him. Then my sergeant knocked on the door to the commanding officer's office and went in.

"Just wait here for a couple of minutes, please," the other sergeant told me. "The colonel will be right with you."

"Sure," I said. The two privates who had "accompanied" me stayed where they were, one on either side of me, standing at parade rest. I wondered if they were hoping I'd make a break for it so they could shoot me down.

The door to the C.O.'s office opened; my sergeant came out and said, "Step in here, please."

"You guys can go," I said to the two privates. "I'll call if I need you."

I walked across the room and into the inner office of the commander of Fort Sills.

The man seated behind the desk was a colonel, but he couldn't have been more than thirty-two, thirty-three years old. This was an unusual position for such a young officer to be in, commanding an installation such as Fort Sills and its surrounding reservation, not to mention dealing with the raids of Quanah Parker and his braves.

"You may go, sergeant," the officer said.

"Yes, sir," the non-com replied, and left the room, shutting the door behind him.

"Mr. Adams?" he said.

"Yes."

"My name is Colonel Mackenzie, sir, Colonel Ronald Mackenzie. I command this installation."

"Very impressive, colonel."

"What is impressive to you, Mr. Adams?" he asked.

"The fact that a man so young would be command of an installation like this, colonel."

I had meant the remark as a compliment, but he seemed to take it as an insult. It appeared that the young colonel did not like to be reminded of his youth, and did not take it well when he was.

"I'm sure my ability to command and my accomplishments speak for themselves, Mr. Adams. General Grant himself assigned me to this command, and I'm sure I've more than justified his confidence in me." He was preening as he spoke, obviously proud of himself.

"I'm sure you have, colonel," I replied.

"Now, as I understand it, Mr. Adams, you took it upon yourself to interfere with three of my men while they were attempting to arrest one of the reservation Comanches—"

"Arrest?" I asked, somewhat stunned. "Is that what you call it when three grown men, soldiers in the United States Army, try to rape a twelve-year-old Indian girl?"

Mackenzie regarded me very calmly and said, "I was

warned that you might bring such an allegation against my men, Mr. Adams."

"Allegation?"

"I understand that the girl's clothing was torn as they attempted to apprehend her. Perhaps you did assume that there was something other than a lawful arrest going on, and for that reason I am not going to place you under arrest."

"Arrest?" I asked, almost choking on the word. "Me?"

"Yes, Mr. Adams. I can't allow private citizens to interfere with the performance of the military—"

"Even when that performance includes rape, and child molestation?" I demanded.

"Mr. Adams," Mackenzie said, his tone becoming extremely cold, "I'll have to ask you not to make such accusations against my men without some sort of evidence to back it up."

"I've got evidence," I told him. "That little girl."

"You mean, that Comanche?" he said, and his tone betrayed what his feelings were about Comanches, whether they were braves, women or even children. "I'm afraid anything she'd have to say would be somewhat biased, wouldn't you say?"

"And your men—they weren't . . . biased?"

"My men are soldiers in the United States Army, Mr. Adams, and I am obliged to accept their word as such over that of a savage, no matter what the age."

"I see," I replied. "Colonel, can I ask what the little girl was being arrested for?"

"You insist on referring to her as a 'little girl,' Mr. Adams. I've seen men who have had their stomachs slit open by twelve-year-old Comanches."

"I'm sure you have," I said. "Could you tell me what the charge was against her?"

"Stealing."

"And what did she steal?"

"A chicken."

"A chicken?" I repeated. *"A whole chicken?"*

"Stealing food is a serious offense for these savages, Adams," he said, dropping any pretense of politeness.

"I'm sure it is. Tell me, is she still subject to arrest?"

"Of course."

"What if she paid for the chicken?"

He laughed derisively and said, "With what?"

"Well, your soldiers had some ideas about that."

"Adams—"

"Please, Colonel. If she paid—"

"If she paid I would be inclined to drop the charges," he said very quickly, as if that eventuality would never arise. "Now, I hope I've made myself—"

"How much?" I asked.

"I beg your pardon?"

"I said, how much for the chicken?"

He stared at me for a moment, as if he didn't understand my question.

"Do I understand you correctly?" he asked finally. "You want to pay for the chicken?"

"You understand correctly, colonel," I said, taking out some money. I produced a dollar and threw it on his desk and asked, "Do you think that would be enough?"

It was more than enough, and he knew it. He stared at the money for a moment, then he picked it up and stared at it.

"That's quite enough, Mr. Adams," he said.

"I expect, then, that you will let your men know that there is no more reason for them to, ah, arrest the little girl?"

I knew that it would bother him when I said "little girl," which was why I insisted on continuing to use that phrase.

He tightened his lips and said, "Yes, I will let them know."

"Thank you," I said. "May I go now?"

"I want to know that you understand my position, Mr. Adams," he said coldly. "If you should take it upon yourself to further interfere with my men in the performance of their duties—"

"As long as those duties don't include roughing up children, colonel, you can rely on me to keep my nose out of Army business," I assured him.

He stared at me for several seconds and then said, "Get out of my office, Adams, and out of Fort Sills at your earliest opportunity. Understood?"

"Oh, I understand, colonel," I said, "perfectly. I assure you, I can't wait to get out of Fort Sills . . . at my earliest opportunity."

"See that you do," he said.

I turned for the door and then stopped before leaving to give one parting shot.

"Oh, colonel."

"What?"

"I'm sure General Grant would be proud to know about the fine job you and your men are doing here." I winked at him. "Fine job," I said again, and left.

Chapter Four

I walked back through the compound, and I was the center of attention. Apparently the word had spread on me, and everybody in that fort wanted to let me know that they had their eye on me. As soon as I left the C.O.'s office, I spotted the sergeant and his two corporal friends. They didn't say anything or make a move towards me, but somehow they let the rest of the men in the fort know that I was the one who had ruined their fun, and I guess from that moment on, I was marked.

It was enough to make a man feel downright lonesome.

I started back to the saloon for another beer—especially since I hadn't finished the first one—but I was brought up short by the touch of a hand on my arm. It was a gentle touch, and the hand was small, so I turned around easily to see who it was.

It was a little Indian girl, about twelve years old. The last time I had seen her, she'd been half-naked and spreadeagled on the ground, about to be taken by three of the U.S. Army's finest.

"Well, hello," I said, smiling at her. She had a dirty face, but underneath the sweat and grime, she was really very pretty.

She grabbed my hand and proceeded to yank on my arm.

"You want me to come with you?" I asked.

She didn't answer, just kept pulling on my arm.

"Okay," I said, "lead on."

She pulled and this time I went along with her. We traveled the long way around and eventually we were among the teepees of the reservation. I got some hard stares from some of the young braves; otherwise I was pretty much ignored. The girl trotted along ahead of me, apparently taking me home with her. Maybe her parents wanted to thank me for saving her virtue.

She stopped in front of one of the many teepees and waited for me to catch up. When I did, she pulled back the flap and waved me in, grinning. I smiled back, ducked my head, and went inside.

Inside there was only one person. It was a girl, and she appeared to be an older version—by maybe five or six years—of the youngster. She had long, black, lustrous hair, dark skin and eyes, a full-lipped mouth, full, rounded breasts and a slim waist. There didn't seem to be a smile within miles of her lovely face, and that was a downright shame.

"Hello," I greeted.

"What are you called?" she asked in excellent English.

"Clint Adams," he said.

"I am Dancing Fawn," she said. "My sister is Dancing Willow. You helped her to get away from the soldiers when they would have soiled her. For that I must thank you."

She was wearing an ornate blanket over her shoulders, and when she released it with her hands it fell to the floor, leaving her totally naked.

She was incredibly lovely. Her skin was superb, smooth and flawless, her breasts round, with very dark nipples. The pubic thatch between her legs was curly, and very black. Her thighs and calves were slim, but well-muscled.

I walked to her and stood directly in front of her. She gazed boldly into my eyes, holding her chin high and proud. Under any other circumstances I would have taken her right there and then.

I bent over and heard her catch her breath. I sneaked a peek at her face and saw that she had closed her eyes. Brave little Indian, I thought, smiling to myself. I picked up the blanket that had gathered around her feet, drew it back up and over her shoulders. She took the ends in her hands again and held it around her.

"You do not want my thanks?" she asked.

"Sure, I do," I answered. "But saying it is enough for me."

She frowned, pulled the blanket tighter around her, and said, "You are a strange man."

"Maybe," I said, "but I've met stranger. I would keep your little sister close by, Dancing Fawn."

"Are the soldiers still looking for her?"

"No—not for that chicken, anyway. I paid for it."

"You paid for the chicken?" she asked, frowning again. "Why did you do this?"

"I don't like to see young girls manhandled, I guess," I answered.

"Even if they are Comanche, and the men are white soldiers?" she asked.

"Especially then." I touched her cheek and said, "We are friends now, Dancing Fawn. I will be here at Fort Sill for a day or so, staying at the hotel." At least, I hoped they had a hotel. "If you have any trouble, you come looking for me. As long as I'm here, I will help you."

"I will remember, Clint Adams," she told me. "I will always remember."

Chapter Five

I started for the saloon and that beer again, but it wasn't to be. As I approached the front door, I spotted the liveryman coming from the other direction.

"Hey, my team ready already?" I asked him.

"I been looking for you, mister," he said.

"Yeah, what for?"

"It's about your team, and your rig."

"What about them?"

"They've been confiscated."

"What?"

"There were some soldiers sniffing around, and they told me to tell you to plan on being in Fort Sill for a while."

I started to ask him why, then changed my question.

"What's your name?" I asked him. He was a small man, about five-three or so, and was probably about my age.

"Freddie."

"Got time for a beer, Freddie?" I asked him.

"And some questions?"

"If you don't mind."

He thought a moment, then said, "Nah, I don't mind. Not as long as the beer is on you."

We went inside and I ordered two beers. When I got

25

them we sat at one of the tables and I asked him about Duke.

"They didn't say nothing about him. I guess they figure you won't leave without your rig and team."

"They're right. What's the story, Freddie? What is it about my rig that would interest the army?"

"I guess it must be all them guns you got inside," he offered.

"The guns. Why?"

He paused a moment and drank some beer.

"Somebody's been selling guns to the Comanches, Mr. Adams," he said.

"Call me Clint," I said. So that was it. Somebody was supplying the Indians with guns, and along comes Clint Adams with a wagon full of guns. I wondered, though, if they would have even checked out my rig if it hadn't been for the incident with the three soldiers that morning. First Mackenzie "suggests" I leave town, and now the Army was holding my property to make me stay around. It seemed that the young colonel had a hard time making up his mind one way or the other.

"Quanah Parker's been riding again, ever since the Army cut loose those Comanches they were holding."

"Why'd they cut them loose?"

"When they captured them, Quanah stopped his raids. I guess they figured he was ready for peace, so they let them go. Now they know they made a mistake. Quanah's raids have started again, and they're worse than ever."

"What kind of guns do they have?" I asked.

"They brought a few of them in the other day. Took them off of some dead braves. I heard tell they were the new Winchester Seventy-threes."

I pursed my lips and whistled soundlessly. The Winchester 73 was the newest, most accurate repeating rifle on the market. It was the first repeating rifle to feature center-fire ammunition, and in the hands of an army of Comanches . . . Well, it was a chilling thought.

"I haven't got any Seventy-threes in my wagon," I said. "Too new."

"Don't tell me, tell them," Freddie said, finishing his beer.

"I think I will, Freddie," I said, "but tomorrow. I don't think the young colonel and I could have a civil conversation right now. We've already had one too many today, as it is."

"Crossed swords with Mackenzie already, huh?" he asked. "There's a young guy who's got everything," he remarked, "including a great big chip on his shoulder. Anybody else'd be glad to be a colonel at his age. Him, he's pissed 'cause he ain't president yet."

"He's a bright boy," I said, "he just might make it. Another beer?"

"Maybe later. Gotta get back to work."

"Where's my rig, Freddie?"

"Locked inside the fort, in their stable. But your black is still in my place."

He got up and I said, "Okay, Freddie, thanks for the information."

"Sure, Mr.—sure, Clint, any time."

"Has this town got a hotel?" I asked.

"Sure, go out and make a left. End of the street."

"Thanks again."

When he left I had a second beer and then went looking for the hotel.

As I signed the register I asked the clerk, "Any law in this town?"

"There's a sheriff," he said. He looked both ways before adding, "He ain't worth much, though. The military is really in charge, he just runs in drunks and Indians."

"Indians?"

"Yea. Them savages ain't allowed inside the town line."

I thought of the little girl who had come to bring me

to her sister. She'd taken a chance then, coming in town.

"Got a preference?" he asked.

"What?"

"I said, you got a preference? You want a room in the front, or the back?"

"Let me have one up front, overlooking the street," I told him.

"Sure. We got plenty of them," he said, handing me a key.

"Business is bad, huh?"

"When ain't it?" he replied. "Especially with all them savages camped right outside the town. Can't wait until they move them."

"To where?"

"Who knows? Anywhere's fine with me—anywhere else, that is," he added. He was an old-timer, about sixty, real thin and pale.

"What's your name?" I asked him.

"Folks 'round here call me Pop, Pop Jordan."

"Okay, Pop. Thanks for the room."

"You're payin' for it," he pointed out. "Ain't nothing to thank me for."

He went back to doing whatever he was doing before I came in, and I went up to my room.

Chapter Six

I dropped my saddlebags off in the room, and then went looking for a bath. The old-timer showed me where there was an old tub, and I had to haul and heat my own water, but it was worth it to feel human again. Once I had my clothes changed, I went looking for the sheriff's office.

There was a plaque on the outside of the office that said: Sheriff Andy Tyler. I walked in and found Tyler sitting behind his desk, trying to build a house of cards with unsteady hands. Next to him was a half-empty bottle of rotgut.

"Sheriff Tyler?" I asked.

He looked up and frowned at the interruption.

"I'm busy, young fella," he said, and went back to his cards.

Tyler was an emaciated man of about forty-five, with gaunt, hollowed-out cheeks and a hawk nose. His eyes were red and watery.

"Sheriff, I'd like to ask you a few questions, if you don't mind."

"Well, I do. I almost got this thing finished, and I ain't about to stop now."

I walked over to the desk, inspected the house of cards, picked out the most crucial card, and then plucked it out from beneath the rest. The whole thing shook and then crumbled, and Tyler's chin actually quivered as he stared at the mass of fallen cards.

"You didn't have to do that," he muttered, reaching for the bottle.

"I want to ask you some questions," I said, grabbing the bottle before he could.

He stared sullenly at the bottle in my hand, and then said, "So ask."

"What's the law hereabouts concerning the reservation Indians?"

"I don't know what you mean."

"Can an Indian bring charges against a white man?" I asked.

"Shit, no. Where'd you get a crazy idea like that?" he asked.

It turned out that one question was enough. I couldn't bring myself to stay in the same room with him any longer. As an ex-lawman, I felt he was an insult to the badge.

"Forget it," I said. "Here, have a ball."

I gave him back the bottle and walked out.

It was getting dark and my stomach was starting to rumble. I looked around and found a small café with good smells coming from it. I went in and ordered a steak, some potatoes, and fresh baked bread. I followed that with a couple of pots of strong black coffee, and then I went looking for something to do. I figured if anybody would know what was doing in town, it would be Freddie.

I went to the livery and found him there.

"Hello, Clint."

"Hi, Freddie. Listen, I was wondering, is there a game anywhere in town?"

"Poker?"

"Preferably."

He rubbed his jaw and said, "Well, there is a game, but . . ."

"But what?"

"It's high stakes," he said.

"So?"

"And you're gonna find some soldiers there, Clint," he added.

"Where does a soldier get the money to play high-stakes poker?" I asked.

"I don't know, and I never ask, but if you go, I'd be careful. You're not too popular with the Army, you know."

"I know."

"I heard about this morning."

"So?"

"What the hell made you butt in, anyway?" he asked, curiosity getting the best of him.

"I don't like seeing three grown men rape a baby, that's why," I replied testily.

"Rape?"

"That's what they were getting ready to do," I said.

"That ain't the story that's going around town," he said.

"That figures."

"Listen, Clint, those three guys you tangled with, they're kind of tough, you know?"

"They didn't seem so tough this morning."

"Well, anyway, they're mean, so be careful. I don't suppose anybody's told you their names?"

"No."

"Well, the sergeant, that's Joe Teal, he's the meanest one. The other two just follow his lead. Sam Brady and Jack Clinch. They're the same, those two."

"I'll watch it. Thanks, Freddie."

"There's one more, Clint, a fourth member of that dirty bunch."

"Who's that?"

"His name's Dutch Black."

"What's he look like?"

Freddie rolled his eyes and said, "You'll know him when you see him, Clint. If you have any trouble with Dutch, just flat out shoot him, and then get out of the way before he falls on you."

"Okay, Freddie, thanks. Now, how about that game?"

Chapter Seven

The game was being held underneath the undertaker's office. The undertaker wasn't playing, he was just cutting the pot. I told him Freddie sent me, and he showed me how to get downstairs. Nobody looked up, because if I didn't belong there, I wouldn't have been passed by the undertaker.

There were a couple of tables going, with five men at one, and six at the other. There were a couple of men standing around, and they were wearing Army uniforms. I recognized one as either Sam Brady or Jack Clinch. Seated at the six-man table was Sergeant Joe Teal. I didn't know the other soldier.

I walked past that table, directly behind one of the corporals, who didn't see me.

"Mind if I sit in?" I asked at the five-man table, indicating the empty chair. The general consensus what that if I could pay, I could play.

From where I sat I could see Joe Teal's profile. If he turned his head to his right, he'd be able to see me, too, and then the fun would start. He appeared to be a good poker player, though, which meant that he concentrated on his cards, and the cards and faces of the other players at his table. I was there for an hour before Brady Clinch happened to look over my way and spot me. He leaned over and whispered something into Teal's ear, but Teal still didn't turn to look at me. He said something in return and, with a last, lingering look at me, the corporal left the room.

I wondered at the time if he were going for reinforcements.

After about four hours, the number of players had thinned out and we consolidated into one table of five. Among those five was Joe Teal.

He already had good reason to dislike me, and the fact that we consistently went head to head and he came out second didn't help matters much. It seemed like every time he had a straight, I had a flush, and every time he had a flush I had a full house. One time he tried to bluff me out with a pair of tens, and I beat him with a pair of Jacks.

After that particular hand, both Brady and Clinch walked in, and with them was one of the biggest men I'd ever seen. This had to be Dutch Black, and I could see what Freddie meant by shoot him and then get out of the way. If he fell on you, he'd kill you, too, by crushing the life out of you. It would be like chopping down an oak tree and then letting it fall on you.

I ignored the three standing soldiers and concentrated on my hand, but not so the other players. The presence of Dutch Black seemed to have dampened their enthusiasm for cards, and after that hand they wanted to call it a night. I didn't mind, since I had come out the big winner.

As the other three players got up to leave, Joe Teal sat back and looked at me. "Adams," he said, "me and my friends would like you to stay a little while longer."

"Is that so?" I said, unbuttoning my shirt. I kept one hand on the table while I used the other one to produce the little .22 New Line from inside my shirt, where I had gotten in the habit of keeping it hidden. I held the gun under the table and pointed it at Teal's stomach. If that big monster made a step towards me, Teal was going to catch some lead in his belly.

"What's it about?" I asked, as the other players filed past Dutch Black and left. Black shut the door behind them and then took up position in front of it, with his arms folded in front of him.

"It's about guns, Adams," Teal said. "We want to know why you're selling guns to Quanah Parker."

"Who?"

"Quanah Parker," he said again. "Don't play games. You know who Quanah is."

"Sounds like an Indian," I said. "Would that be a good guess?"

"He's a funny man, Joe," one of the corporals said.

I looked at him and asked, "Which one are you? Clinch or Brady."

He looked surprised, but he said, "I'm Clinch." He was the one who had been standing behind Teal when I first entered the room.

"That makes you Brady," I said to the other one, "and the big ugly one is Dutch Black, right?"

"I may be ugly," Dutch Black said in a deep voice, "but I could make you a whole lot uglier."

He had a massive jaw and remarkably small eyes for a man his size. He stood about six-six, six-seven or so, with arms that were longer than my legs.

"Not yet, Dutch," Joe Teal said, but he was looking at me when he said it.

"Not ever, Teal," I said. "Tell him to move aside. I'm leaving, now."

I picked up my money with my empty hand and stuffed it into my shirt pocket.

"No, you're not, Adams," Teal said.

"Yes, I am, Teal," I said. When I was sure that it was quiet enough in the room for him to hear it, I cocked the hammer on the .22, and I saw him stiffen. His eyes became shifty and started to blink.

"Tell him to move away from the door to the other side of the room," I instructed again.

"Do it, Dutch," Teal said aloud.

The big man hesitated, giving me a murderous look, but he finally ambled over to the other side of the room.

"Now the other two monkeys," I told Teal.

"Hey—" Clinch started, but Teal interrupted him.

"Shut up, Clinch. Both of you, move."

"He won't shoot, Joe," Clinch said.

"Okay," Teal replied. "When he's got the gun pointed at your belly, Jack, you can call his bluff. Right now you and Sam move over by Dutch, all right?"

Clinch and Brady did as their sergeant said, and when they were all on the other side of the room Teal said, "Now what?"

"Now you stand between me and them, Joe," I said, standing up.

Teal looked at the gun in my hand and laughed without humor.

"Go ahead, Joe," I said. "Try it. It'll kill you just as dead as a forty-four."

He stared at me a moment, then nodded to himself and got up.

"Between me and your friends," I said again.

He backed up until he was standing halfway between us, and then I moved for the door.

"We're gonna test you with Dutch, Adams," he said to me.

"You send him after me, Joe," I said, "and I'll put a bullet between his eyes. After that, I'll come after you."

"Before you go—" Teal said as I opened the door.

"What?"

"—the C.O. wants to see you in his office in the morning."

"About what?"

He smiled and said, "About guns, I guess."

"That's okay," I assured him. "I want to see him, too. Thanks for the game."

Chapter Eight

In the morning I had a leisurely breakfast, with my requisite two pots of coffee, and then went to talk to Colonel Ronald Mackenzie about guns.

"I have an appointment with the colonel," I told his sergeant.

"Yes, sir. Would you wait one moment, please?" the young sergeant asked me. He was Mackenzie's secretary, of that I was sure. Probably got promoted by Mackenzie and seated at that desk. By the time he became an officer, he wouldn't know diddlyshit about what it was like to be in the field, let alone be in command in the field.

But he knew how to be polite.

"Since you asked so nice," I said, "I'll wait."

He looked at me funny, said, "Uh, yes," and went into the colonel's office. He came out in a few moments and said, "The colonel will see you, now, sir."

"Thank you, sergeant," I said, and walked past him.

"Sit down, Adams," he said without looking up.

"I'll stand," I replied. "What the hell is the idea of confiscating my rig?"

Now he looked up at me and said, "You are the subject of a military investigation, Mr. Adams, to determine whether or not you have been selling guns to the Indians."

"Goddammit, colonel, that's bull and you know it. I've only been in Texas a couple of days."

"You've been in Fort Sill for one day, Adams, that's all I know. Where you were before that, I have no way of knowing. You could have been out on the Staked Plains, selling Quanah Parker Winchester Seventy-threes."

"Colonel, you've got no cause to believe that," I said.

"Don't I?" he asked. "You come riding in here with a wagon full of guns, and the first thing you do is interfere with three of my soldiers as they are attempting to arrest a Comanche."

"You're still calling what they did—"

"It doesn't matter what you thought they were doing!" he shouted at me. "You stepped in and took the side of a Comanche against your own kind! That makes you suspect."

"When did you come out here?" I asked him.

The question caught him off guard, and he answered it honestly.

"I was assigned here in 1871, for the express purpose of stopping Quanah Parker—"

"—and after two years, you still haven't done so," I finished. "I think it's gone to your head, colonel."

"Adams, you had better be careful how you talk to me!" he warned me stridently. "I'll bury you and your property so deep in army red tape that you'll never be seen again."

I started to reply with a threat of my own, but bit it back and changed my tack.

"How long do you intend to keep me here?" I asked.

"As long as our investigation takes. Cooperate, and you'll be gone sooner than you think."

"Or else I'll be under arrest on some trumped-up charge," I added.

"If you're guilty, you'll be arrested, Adams," he said,

"and it won't be on any trumped-up charge."

"Have you inventoried my property yet?"

"Not yet."

"Well, you'll notice that there are no Winchester Seventy-threes in my stock."

"Your stock?"

"Guns are my business, colonel. I repair them, I make them, sometimes I sell them—but not to Quanah Parker, and not anything remotely resembling a new Winchester Seventy-three."

Tapping his fingers on his desk top he said, "That remains to be seen. Where are you staying?"

"Where else is there to stay?" I asked.

"The hotel? Very well, then. I'll be in touch."

"Yeah," I said, standing up. "Oh, yes, one more thing."

"What's that?"

"Joe Teal."

"What about Sergeant Teal?" he asked.

"If he and his friends are going to keep pushing me, I can't be responsible for what happens," I told him.

"Sergeant Teal is one of my finest men," he said. "You interfered with his duty, and he is not likely to forget that."

"His *duty*. He doesn't know the meaning of that word."

I stared at the young colonel, who was staring back at me very calmly. I wanted to tell him something that would shake him up, but I was never one to trade on my reputation, which I had acquired in spite of myself. "The Gunsmith" some newspaperman had called me years ago, and it had stuck. Of course, there was the chance that the colonel already knew who I was, and felt secure that he had the entire U.S. Army behind him, but somehow I didn't think that was the case.

"If you investigate me, Colonel Mackenzie," I said,

standing up, "you had better do a damned good job of it."

"What do you mean?" he asked.

I walked to the door and said from there, "All I mean is that before you take someone on, you should make sure who it is you're taking on."

Chapter Nine

I wanted to take my own advice, which meant I had to find out everything I could about Colonel Ronald Mackenzie. I was sure that it wasn't the entire U.S. Army I was taking on, but Ronald Mackenzie himself—and his henchman. Mackenzie hated Comanches, and the fact that I had gone against his men on behalf of a Comanche girl stuck in his craw.

The best source of information in Fort Sill appeared to be my friend Freddie, who was quite free with it for the price of a beer. That was all it took to lure him away from his livery.

With a cold brew sitting in front of him he asked, "How'd you do at the game last night?"

"Not too bad," I answered. "By the way, I met Dutch Black."

"And you're still walking around? He must have been by himself. He can't think when he's alone. Joe Teal thinks for him."

"Teal was there, too. In fact, I took quite a few dollars of Teal's money from him."

He shook his head and said, "Clint, you're really making an enemy for yourself, there. Joe Teal fancies himself a real good poker player. What happened?"

"Nothing. We played some cards, had a chat, and

then I left them there. No real problem at all."

He frowned at me as if he had a hard time believing that.

"Listen, Freddie, I need some information, and I figure you're the man to get it from."

"What kind of information?" he asked. "About who?"

"Colonel Ronald Mackenzie."

He gave a long sigh and said, "He's bad news, Clint. Rules this fort with an iron hand."

"Discipline doesn't seem to be that hard," I commented. "Not from what I've seen, anyway."

"Well, you've seen Mackenzie's crew of Teal, Brady, Clinch and Dutch Black. With the rest of the men it's by the book."

"I see. He's been here—what—two years?"

He nodded.

"Came here in seventy-one to stop Quanah, and them two have been going at it ever since. That man hates Indians in general, and Comanches in particular—and you can't be too high on his list either, Clint."

"Why's that?"

"He'd have you pegged as an Indian lover, right about now. That's why he's hassling you about your rig."

"Where does he live?" I asked.

"He's in one of those houses out behind town," Freddie answered. "Lives there with his wife."

"He's married?"

"He sure is," he answered, and a dreamy kind of look came into his eyes. "In fact, the only good thing about the colonel is his wife. What a beauty she is."

"Is that a fact?"

"It is. She's blonde, young—"

"How young?"

"A good ten years younger than him, I'd say. He

keeps her hidden out there at his house. I think he's afraid to let her into town, but she comes in every once in a while to go shopping. My, but does she draw stares when she walks down the street, I tell you. The colonel usually has someone come in with her."

"One of Teal's men?" I asked.

"Not usually," he answered, "although Dutch Black has come in with her once or twice, but I think that was when she was going on some kind of a shopping spree and needed Dutch to carry all of the packages."

"So the colonel is young, ambitious, has a beautiful wife and hates Indians."

"That's about it."

"Is he a brave man?" I asked.

"You mean physically brave?" he asked. "I don't know. He goes out in the field pretty often, but that's with a bunch of troopers behind him. He was wounded a while back, but not bad. Took an arrow in his hip when they captured all them Indians."

"Whose decision was it to let them go?" I asked.

"Not Mackenzie's. He wanted to shoot them all. He got orders from Washington to let them go as a show of good faith." Freddie laughed and said, "What a mistake that was. I bet nobody's admitting to that decision."

"Okay, Freddie, thanks a lot." I got up and threw some coins on the table. "Have another on me, okay?"

"There's more than enough here for one more beer," he pointed out.

"I know," I said. "I'll be seeing you."

I left the saloon and headed for the telegraph office, which I'd seen near the livery. I wanted to do some further checking on Colonel Mackenzie, so I'd know for sure who I was taking on, and it seemed to me that Washington was the best place to check.

"I'd like to send a telegram," I told the thin man behind the counter at the telegraph office.

"Sure," he said. He pushed a pad and pencil towards me and said, "Just write what you want to say on that there piece of paper, mister."

"Thanks."

I had a friend in Washington who was a captain in the army, and I simply addressed the telegram to him and asked him for a personal recommendation of Colonel Ronald Mackenzie, assigned to Fort Sill, Texas.

When I signed my name and pushed it back at the man he counted the words and told me how much I owed him. After I paid him he seemed to look at my signature as an afterthought, and when he saw my name his expression froze.

It was obvious that he had recognized my name, and there were a couple of explanations for that. He could simply have recognized it from my reputation, or someone could have already been there sending a telegram about me, and he had seen the answer, as well as the man who sent it.

Colonel Mackenzie had not allowed any grass to grow under his feet. By now he must have known who I was. He knew I was not just a drifter, or a gun salesman.

Now, I don't mean to imply that it was just my reputation with a gun that was going to make the colonel tread a little lighter when dealing with me. There was also the fact that I had been a lawman—a town sheriff as well as a deputy federal marshall—for eighteen years before giving up my badge. He had to assume that I knew who was federally connected, and that meant that he would also have to assume that I might have occasion to send a telegram to someone.

"When can I expect an answer on this?" I asked the man behind the counter.

He regarded me warily from behind his wire frame glasses and said, "I will try to have an answer for you as soon as possible, Mr. Adams, sir."

"I'll be at the hotel or the saloon," I told him. "Make sure you find me as soon as my answer comes in."

"Yes, sir."

When I left the office, however, I did not hold out much hope of getting an answer. The colonel would either have made sure that none of my telegrams would get out, or he would let them go through and monitor my requests, and my answers. Which was the case would remain to be seen.

On the way back to my hotel I passed the saloon-cum-general store, and I went in and ordered some supplies, mostly dried meats, flour, corn meal, sugar, and other dried foods. I also got some bacon and bread.

"Put it in a sack," I told the clerk, and he did as I asked. I paid him and tossed the sack over my shoulder.

I figured that by now that stolen chicken must be gone, and Dancing Fawn and Dancing Willow must be getting hungry again. The way Dancing Fawn had looked, offering herself to me, naked, was still plain in my mind, so my reasons for bringing this food to them were not altogether unselfish.

Besides which, if Mackenzie found out about it, it would make him even madder at me than he was.

For some reason, the madder I thought of him getting, the better I felt.

Chapter Ten

I went the long way around again, because there was no use in challenging the entire post, and after a little difficulty I managed to find Dancing Fawn's teepee.

"Dancing Fawn?" I called out. Once again I had gotten some dirty looks from some of the younger bucks, but for the most part had been ignored.

When I called out again, the flap of the teepee was thrown back and the little one, Dancing Willow, peeked out. When she saw me she smiled widely and beckoned me to come in. Inside, I found Dancing Willow seated in the center of the teepee. When she saw me she stared, frowning slightly. She must have been wondering what I was doing there.

"Hello, Dancing Fawn."

She didn't answer, just kept staring. Her little sister said something to her in their language, but she answered very shortly and the little girl left.

"What do you wish?" she asked.

"I don't wish anything, Dancing Fawn," I said, putting the sack down on the ground. "I've brought you and your sister something."

She leaned forward and opened the top of the sack to look inside.

"You put us further in your debt," she said, looking up at me.

"I'm not trying to do that, Dancing Fawn. I just want to help you and your sister survive."

"The soldiers will not like it if they should see," she warned me. "You risk the wrath of your own people."

"Those men are not my people, Dancing Fawn, I assure you," I said. "Will you accept my offering?"

She looked in the sack again, and then said, "It would not be fair to the rest of my people for my sister and I to keep these things to ourselves. I will not accept unless I can share them with the rest of my people."

"You may do whatever you wish with them," I said.

"Then I accept, with thanks."

"There is one other thing."

"Yes?"

"Keep your sister close to your teepee, Dancing Fawn. Keep an eye on her. I wouldn't trust those men to stay away from her, just because I paid for the stolen chicken. Do you understand?"

"I understand that you are a special man. My people are grateful."

"I would rather have your friendship," I said.

She regarded me very seriously, and then said, "You have it."

"Good. Dancing Fawn, I would like to come by tomorrow and take you riding."

"Riding?"

"Yes, in a buggy. I would bring some food and we would take a ride and stop somewhere for lunch."

"Why?" she asked.

"Why?" I repeated. "As a token of our new friendship."

"If I do this it means we are friends?" she asked.

It seemed the easiest explanation, so I said, "Yes."

"Then you may come for me tomorrow," she said.

"Good. I will be here in Fort Sill a little longer than I expected, so perhaps we will be able to get to know each other much better."

"I hope that is so," she agreed.

"I will see you tomorrow."

"I will be ready whenever you come," she said.

She had an incredibly lovely face, with those dark eyes, high, prominent cheekbones and wide mouth. Her teeth were straight and white, her neck slim and graceful. Today she wore a short dress made of some animal skin, and it showed off her lovely, trim but powerful legs.

Dancing Willow came running back in at that point and ran right into me.

"Whoa!" I said, catching her so she wouldn't fall. She said something to me in her language, and then went to stand by her sister.

"What did she say?" I asked.

"She says you are the only white man she likes," her older sister translated for me.

"Well, you tell her that I am very honored, and that I like her very much, too."

"I will tell her."

"Goodbye, Dancing Fawn, until tomorrow."

This made twice that I had seen and spoken to Dancing Fawn, and still I had not seen her smile. That was my goal for tomorrow—somehow, during our ride and lunch, to get her to smile.

Chapter Eleven

"Another beer?" the bartender asked.

"No, thanks," I replied. I had already spent most of the day in the saloon, waiting for an answer to my telegram. I paid my bill and left, knowing that I'd probably end up back there again later on in the evening.

Walking the length of the town didn't take very long, and I decided to do it again, which turned out to be a very good decision.

I must have been staring at something inside my head, because I didn't see what was right in front of me—a lady, and a very pretty one. I didn't see her until I practically walked over her, knocking her packages from her hands.

"Oh!" she shouted, and started doing a pretty good juggling act until everything got out of hand.

"I'm sorry," I apologized, and we both bent over to start retrieving the packages from the ground.

"It's all right," she assured me. "No harm done. There's nothing breakable in any of these."

I didn't really take a good look at her face until we stood up, each holding an equal amount of packages.

She had honey-blonde hair and great big, green eyes that were startlingly clear. Her nose was upturned and came to a slight point, and her mouth was full, wide and inviting.

In fact, her entire demeanor was inviting, even when she wasn't meaning to be. Women like that are dangerous—but then all women are dangerous.

That never stopped me before.

Instead of piling the packages back up on her, I said, "Well, the least you could let me do is help you carry them."

She hesitated a moment, then replied, "It would be a help. I do have a bit further to go. Thank you."

We started walking together and she said, "I feel silly, but I'm not quite used to trying to carry all of my own packages. My husband usually sends someone with me to help."

"Your husband?" I asked, trying to hide my disappointment.

"Yes," she said. She stopped walking and turned to face me, giving me the full benefit of those lovely eyes. "Would you like to give those to me, now?"

"Not at all," I answered. "I'm sure no husband could object to a gentleman carrying a lady's packages for her."

She regarded me still for a moment longer, then said, "All right, then. This way."

We stepped off the end of the boardwalk—and the end of the town—and started back towards the houses behind town.

"What does your husband do?" I asked, although I was sure I knew.

"He's a soldier," she said, and there was curious lack of pride in her tone when she said it.

"Just a soldier?" I asked.

She didn't respond immediately. When she did, at last, she said, "No, not just a soldier. He is a colonel, and he is the commanding officer of Fort Sill."

"Colonel Mackenzie," I said.

"Yes."

"And what's your name?"

"Sheila," she answered. I couldn't help feeling that most women would have said, "Sheila Mackenzie," but she chose to leave her last name—or her husband's last name—off.

I had a feeling that this was one married woman who was more herself than her husband's wife.

I had only just met her, but I couldn't picture her married to that baby-faced blowhard, Mackenzie.

"That's quite a position for someone so young," I said.

She stared at me and asked, "How did you know he was young?"

"I wasn't talking about him," I answered.

"Here we are," she announced. We had arrived at a small house, though it was bigger than most of the others. "May I make you a cup of coffee, as a thank you?"

"I'll carry the packages in," I said, "but it might not look very good for you if I stayed more than a few moments. People talk—"

"—and what they say means very little," she put in. "Please, allow me to thank you."

"I'm the one who knocked the packages out of your hands in the first place," I reminded her.

We were stopped right in front of her door, and I would have had to take all of the packages from her so she could unlock it. She carefully placed her armload right on top of mine and said—recklessly, I remember thinking at the time—"Maybe that's what I want to thank you for."

Chapter Twelve

The last place I would have expected to find myself that day—or week, or even month—was in bed with the wife of Colonel Ronald Mackenzie. I took no particular pleasure at being in bed with the colonel's wife, but I felt nothing but pleasure at being there with a girl named Sheila.

We had walked into the house and I had put down the packages. We looked at each other for a few moments, and all thoughts of coffee vanished. She walked into her bedroom, and I followed.

When she had removed all of her clothing she stood there for me to inspect. Her breasts were full and round, topped by pink nipples. Her waist was that of a very young girl, but her hips were a woman's—and her face was an angel's, with the sun streaming through the window and creating a halo from her hair.

There was no illusion of love there. I've never believed in love without knowing someone, and I didn't know Sheila Mackenzie, but at that moment I didn't know myself, either. I felt nervous, and it had nothing to do with the fact that I was in Colonel Ronald Mackenzie's house, about to take his wife into his bed. It had only to do with her.

She sat on the bed and watched me as I undressed, and I had never been watched as closely before by any other woman. Her eyes followed every move, took in every inch of me, as if she were committing me to memory.

It made me think that there was only going to be this once, and that she wanted to remember every moment.

When I touched her she shivered, but it was not from any feeling of cold. Her nipples blossomed immediately, and she lay back with me beside her. We didn't speak, not the whole time that we made love.

Her skin was pale, warm, smooth and soft. As I kissed her breasts and sucked her nipples, the touch of her fingers on my back was light, yet insistent. She barely touched me, yet with her touch she urged me on. I explored her entire body with my mouth, and when I nestled between her legs, she entwined my hair in her fingers and moaned aloud. She reached the point of no return and cried out, "Oh, yes," and those were the only words spoken by either one of us the whole time we were in bed together.

I rose above her and with her hands she found my erection. She opened herself up for me and I sank all the way into her warmth and wetness. She wrapped her legs around me; her legs and thighs were strong and firm. I reached beneath her to cup her behind in my hands and she was content to let me set the tempo as we thrust at each other. I made it last so long that it became painful for me, and still I made it last, until I thought my whole body would explode. When I finally emptied myself into her, she held me to her tightly, as if she was afraid to let go. Her face was buried in my neck, her mouth against my skin, and as she moaned with pleasure it seemed to set off vibrations in my body.

I'd had many, many women before Sheila Mackenzie. I'd had some who were as good, some not as good, and I'd had a few who were better, but on the whole I had never had an experience that quite matched that one.

Chapter Thirteen

"This has never happened before," she said afterward.

"It's never happened to me quite this way, either," I was forced to admit.

"No, I mean, I've never . . . done that with anyone but my husband before."

"I see," I said. "I suppose I should be flattered."

We were sitting at her kitchen table, having that cup of coffee she'd offered me earlier. Neither of us thought it very prudent to remain in her bed and take a chance on her husband walking in on us.

Now she shook her head and said, "We didn't play word games before, Clint, so let's not play any now."

"All right," I agreed. "We saw each other and wanted each other. I guess it happens that way sometimes. There's no harm done, and there's no reason to think it will ever happen again."

"I want it to happen again," she said. "You do, too."

"I suppose you're right."

"Have you met my husband?" she asked.

"I've had that dubious pleasure," I said, and then related to her the circumstances of our two meetings.

"You've seen Ronald flex his muscles, then," she said. "I don't suppose you were any more impressed than I am."

"I suppose he impresses his men," I said.

"Some of them," she agreed. Then she added, "Most of them."

"What about Teal, and his friends?"

She shuddered.

"Ronald's changed since he took up with them," she said. "He's changed since we came here. When I saw him start to change, I begged him to leave, but he wouldn't hear of it. General Grant sent him here to do a job, he said, and he was going to do it," she said in disgust.

"Why don't you leave on your own?" I asked.

"I've thought about it," she said. "I really have, but I believe that Ronald would kill me first . . . unless . . ."

"Unless what?"

"Unless a better man than him took me away," she said.

I looked at her and said, "That's a lot to ask of a man on a moment's notice, Sheila."

She smiled grimly and said, "I'm not asking you to love me, Clint, just take me with you when you leave. Think about it."

"I will," I said, draining my coffee cup, "but it might be some time before I can leave, myself."

"Whenever," she said. "I've been waiting two years, I can wait a little longer."

"All right," I said. "Now that we've got that settled, tell me something about your husband."

"Like what?"

"If I face him, will he back down, or will he face up to me?" I asked.

"Neither," she said. "He'll probably send Joe Teal, Dutch Black and the others after you."

"That's what I figured," I said. "Three of them don't worry me."

"Dutch Black?"

I shook my head.

"Joe Teal's the one with the brains. He's the one who worries me. The others follow his lead. If I can take care of him, they won't know what to do."

"Sounds like it makes sense," she said.

"Oh, it does. That's just the way you kill a snake, Sheila. Cut off the head and the body dies."

I stood up to leave and buckled on my gun.

"Ronald is never here during the day," she informed me. "He comes home for dinner after six."

"Does he stay home?"

"Sometimes," she said. "I never know until the time comes."

"I'll come and see you, Sheila."

"Just be careful nobody sees you," she said.

"Oh, you mean, more careful than we were today?"

"You have to take a risk now and then to get what you want," she said. "After that, you watch your step."

"I'll remember that," I said. "I surely will."

Chapter Fourteen

When I left Sheila Mackenzie I went straight to the telegraph office. As I walked in, the little clerk looked as frightened as if I were Quanah Parker himself, all decked out in full war paint.

"Did you get an answer on my telegram yet?" I asked him, leaning against the counter.

"Uh, n-no, sir," he stammered, and I knew that my fears about Mackenzie intercepting my telegram were well-founded.

I leaned over the counter until my nose was inches from his and asked, "Did you even send it?"

"Um, I, uh——" he began to stutter. His eyes were darting back and forth, looking for a way out.

"Never mind," I said, moving back.

"I'm sorry, mister," he said, "but I didn't have anything to say about it. It's a military matter."

"A military matter," I repeated.

"That's what I was told."

"Was it Colonel Mackenzie himself who came and got my telegram?" I asked.

He shook his head.

"It was Sergeant Teal and that, uh, that big fella," he said, holding his hand way above his head.

"Dutch Black."

"That's him," he said. The very thought of Dutch Black frightened him more than my actual presence did.

"Mister Adams, you gotta believe me—" he started to say, but I cut him off.

"What's your name?" I asked him.

"Walter."

"Okay, Walter, forget it. Just tell me one thing?"

"What?" he asked, looking as if I might ask him to remove his right arm and give it to me as an apology.

"Did the sergeant send a telegram while he was here?"

"No," he said.

"No?"

"No. He came in earlier, before you, and sent a telegram."

"Is that so?"

"Yeah. Then when he came in to see if you had tried to send any telegrams, he picked up his answer."

"Which was?"

He stared at me for a moment, and then I had to ask him again. He jumped a bit and then quickly said, "Who you were, he found out who you were."

"Who am I?" I asked him.

"You know."

I smiled at him and said, "Humor me."

"You're the, uh, the Gunsmith."

"You've heard of me?" I asked.

"Yeah, lots of people have."

"Had the sergeant?"

"Sure."

I nodded. Now they knew who I was. It remained to be seen if, for once, my "reputation" would work for me instead of against me.

"Was Sergeant Teal impressed?" I asked.

"Hell, no," he answered. "He seemed to like the idea."

Yeah, I thought he might.

"Okay, Walter, thanks," I said. He looked surprised that I would thank him, and he smiled shakily. I think he was still not sure that I wouldn't draw my gun and plug him before I left.

Somehow I resisted that impulse and left.

I went to the saloon to sit down over a beer and consider my options. I could go to Colonel Mackenzie's office again and demand that he allow my telegrams to go through. Naturally, he'd say no, not while I was under investigation. I could demand again that he release my property. He'd say no, not while I was under investigation.

Another meeting with Mackenzie obviously wouldn't accomplish anything, especially after the tone of our first two.

I was frustrated. Here I was, stuck in Fort Sill by some wet-behind-the-ears colonel who may or may not have actually believed that I was sellling guns to the Indians. He could also be using that as an excuse to give me a hard time because I stood up against *his* men for a *Comanche*. Imagine the nerve of me. . . .

After a second beer I found myself starting to entertain the thought of going out to look for Teal and his boys, just to take my frustrations out on them. I rejected the idea, because in the event that such a confrontation took place, someone would undoubtedly end up dead— one of them, or me.

Neither eventuality was very desirable at the moment.

Instead, I decided to order another beer, and halfway through that one I came up with another option, something that would enable me to leave Fort Sill, free and clear.

All I had to do was find out who really was selling guns to the Comanches. That was easy, right?

Chapter Fifteen

"You have troubles?" Dancing Fawn asked me while we were eating lunch the next day.

"Why do you ask that?"

"You do not talk," she answered simply.

"Well, I thought we were talking," I replied to that.

She shook her head and said, "You do not say what is in your head, about what is weighing heavily on your shoulders."

I stared at her a moment and then said, "You're very perceptive, aren't you?"

"I do not understand that word," she said, frowning.

"You notice things," I explained, "that other people do not notice."

"I know only that you are very troubled," she said. "I do not have to be per—uh—"

"Perceptive," I supplied.

"Yes, I need not be that to know that you are being troubled by something."

"Well, you're right," I said. "There is something on my mind, but—"

"I listen very well," she said, before I could go any further. "You helped my sister and I would like to help you."

"That's very nice, Dancing Fawn, but I don't know that you—"

"Please?"

She wanted so much to repay me for helping her that I decided to go ahead and tell her what was on my mind.

"The military has confisc—uh, has taken my property away from me. My wagon, all of my supplies inside the wagon, and my team of horses."

"Why?"

"Someone has been selling rifles to Quanah Parker, Dancing Fawn. The colonel at the fort seems to think that I may be the one."

"Are you?"

"No. I've never even seen Quanah Parker."

"Then why do you not tell him this?" she asked, puzzled that I would not have taken such a simple way out.

"I did tell him," I answered, "but he has to investigate, find out for himself whether I am or not."

"Why do you not find out who is selling the guns and then tell the colonel?"

"Well, I've just decided that that is exactly what I'm going to have to do," I explained. "Now I just have to figure out how."

Abruptly, she stood up and said, "I will help you."

"You will?" I asked, looking up at her. She appeared very determined to do just that. "How will you do that?"

"I will take you to Quanah."

For a moment I wasn't sure I had heard her right.

"What did you say?"

"I will take you to Quanah," she repeated. "I will tell him how you helped Dancing Willow and me, and he will help you."

"He will? How can you be so sure of that? Why should Quanah Parker help me?"

"Because I will ask him to," she said.

"And just like that he'll agree?"

"Of course."

"Why?" I asked again.

"Come," she said, avoiding the question. "Clean up and we will go."

"Now?"

"It is early. We have time to ride to the Staked Plains. I will find Quanah, and he will help you. Come."

She busied herself cleaning up, and I started to wonder just why Quanah Parker would help me just because Dancing Fawn asked him to.

Chapter Sixteen

The man had been dead for some time—days, possibly even a week. The sun had bloated the body beyond recognition. One thing I had no trouble recognizing, however, was the cause of death.

He had an arrow sticking out of his belly.

"That is a Kwahadi arrow," Dancing Fawn informed me.

"One of Quanah's?"

"It is Kwahadi," she said again.

The ground was hard, but there were signs there that indicated the presence of many horses, and a wagon.

Could this be the man who had been selling the rifles to the Indians? Had they taken his last shipment, and then killed him?

I dismounted and removed a blanket from my bed roll.

"What are you going to do?" she asked.

"I'm going to take the body back to Fort Sill," I answered.

"How?"

"You and I will ride double on my horse, and I'll tie the body to yours. It will take us a while, but we'll get there."

"Do you think this will convince your colonel that

you were not selling guns?" she asked.

"I hope so," I said, rolling the bloated body up in my blanket, which I would burn afterwards.

"You do not want to meet Quanah?"

"It may not be necessary, Dancing Fawn," I told her. "This might just do the trick."

"And if it does not do the trick? You will want to meet Quanah then?" she asked.

"If you're still willing to help me, it would be the only other solution."

She slid down from her horse and said, "I will always be willing to help you, Clint. Come, I will help you lift the body."

And she did, with no trace of distaste at handling it. Together we got it up on her horse and tied down tightly, and I wished we had kept the buggy.

"Let's go," I said, pulling her up behind me on Duke.

When we reached Fort Sill hours later, I left her off before entering the fort.

"You will let me know what happens?" she asked.

"I will. Thank you for your help, Dancing Fawn."

"You will let me know if I can help again?"

"I will."

"Good luck, Clint."

I rode up to the main gates of the fort and was admitted when I stated my name. Once inside, I headed straight for Mackenzie's office.

"I'd like to see the colonel," I told his sergeant.

"What is it about, sir?"

"It's about the rifles that are being sold to the Indians," I answered. I figured that would be the fastest way to get in to see him.

"Wait a minute," the non-com said. He went into his colonel's office for a few moments, then came out and told me, "You can go in, now."

"Thanks," I said, brushing by him.

"Have you come to confess, Adams?" Mackenzie

asked, eyeing me from his seated position behind his desk.

"You'd like that, wouldn't you, colonel. No, I haven't come to confess. I brought you something."

"What?"

"It's outside, tied to a horse."

"Well, what is it?"

"It's a body."

"Whose?" he asked, frowning.

"I was hoping you could tell me that," I said. "All I know is that I found him lying out there with an arrow in his gut."

He started to ask another question, then stopped and called out, "Sergeant!"

When the man came running in Mackenzie instructed him to go out and see to the body that was tied to one of my horses, and try to get an identification of it.

He turned to me when his man went back out and said, "Where did you find him?"

"Out on the Staked Plains."

"The Staked—what the hell were you doing out there? Having a meeting with Quanah?"

"That was the idea," I admitted.

"Wha—" he said, mouth dropping open at what he probably thought was a confession.

"I was going out there to try and find out from Quanah who has been selling him the guns so I could clear myself."

He stared at me for a few seconds, and then said, "You mean you were going to get yourself killed."

"Oh, does that mean you don't think I'm selling Quanah guns? If I was, why would he kill me."

He pointed his finger at me and said, "You're not off the hook yet, Adams."

I was about to answer when there was a knock on the door.

"Come in."

His Sergeant came in and said, "We've identified the body, colonel."

"Well, do you have to make me ask?"

"It's Amos Holt, sir."

"Holt?" Mackenzie asked. "Well, that's no great loss. Thank you, sergeant."

"Yes, sir?"

"The arrow, I'd like the arrow that killed Holt."

"Yes, sir, but it wasn't in the—"

"It's on my horse, Sergeant, the big black," I spoke up.

Mackenzie told his man, "Go and get it."

"Yes, sir."

"It's a Kwahadi arrow," I said as the sergeant left.

"Oh? Are you an expert on such matters?" he asked.

"No, I just happened to have someone with me who is," I explained.

"Who was that?"

"The sister of the little girl your men tried to rape," I answered.

"Now just a minute, Adams—"

"I'm not here to discuss that incident, colonel," I interrupted him. "I brought that man's body in because I thought it would help the both of us." I stood up and added, "I hope that it does."

"We shall see," he said, his tone noncommital.

"Yeah," I replied, "I guess we shall. Oh, one other thing."

"Yes?"

"Who was this guy, Amos Holt?"

"He was half-owner of the saloon and general store."

"Who's the other half?"

"I don't know why I should tell you, but it's Jed Jordan. You might know Jed's father. He owns the hotel."

Chapter Seventeen

I went back to my hotel to clean up after my long ride, and also to ask Jed Jordan's father where I might find him.

"Over at the saloon," the old man said. "He not only owns it, he works in it. He's the bartender."

I tried to remember what he looked like from the few times I'd been there, but the only image I could come up with was that of a very tall, thin man of indeterminate age.

"Thanks," I said to his father.

"Uh, does he owe you money?" the old man asked.

"No, why do you ask?"

He shrugged his thin shoulders and said, "Because he owes a lot of people money, even me. He ain't in a hurry to pay it back, either."

"I'll mention it to him when I see him."

"Won't do no good. I know he's got it, but he won't part with it."

Well, so far I'd found out that Jed Jordan was a lousy son; now I needed to find out what kind of a partner he was.

It was dark when I left the hotel, and as I walked to the saloon, I thought about the body of Amos Holt.

Why else would Holt have been out there but to deal

with Quanah? Then again, I was out there, and I wasn't selling guns. How could I condemn Holt just for being found dead on the Staked Plains?

Still, I'd be very interested in knowing his reason for being out there. Maybe his partner could tell me.

When I reached the saloon it was doing a healthy business, which meant there was at least one person sitting at each of the three wooden tables. I walked up to the bar and ordered a beer from Jed Jordan, and took the opportunity to get a better look at him.

He was as tall and thin as I remembered, but taking a better look at his face, I figured that he was at least forty. His face looked as if some of the people he'd owed money to over the years had taken exception to it—in other words, he'd been hit in the face more than a few times. He wore a Navy Colt tied down on his thigh, and it looked as if it had seen years of hard service.

"Are you Jed Jordan?" I asked him.

He set my beer down and frowned at me, saying, "Yeah, who wants to know?"

"My name's Adams, Clint Adams," I said, picking up the beer. It was cold and tasted good after all of that riding I'd done that day.

"Oh yeah, you're the guy the soldiers took out of here yesterday," he said.

"That's right. I'm staying over in your old man's hotel."

"Good for you," he said, and started to walk away.

"You used to be partners with Amos Holt, didn't you?" I asked him.

"Used to be?" he asked, looking back at me. "What do you mean, 'used to be'?"

"Has he been around lately?"

"Actually, I haven't seen him for a few days. Have you seen him?"

"Oh yes, I have. In fact, I found him and brought him in today."

"What do you mean, found him?" he asked, turning to face me. "If you've got something to say, mister, say it plain." His tone had become as nasty as his face.

"I found your partner with an arrow sticking out of his gut," I said. "Is that plain enough for you?"

"Amos is dead?" he asked, looking as if the thought did not distress him a whole lot. "Where'd that happen?"

"Out on the Staked Plains."

"Quanah's country?" he asked. "I knew it!" he snapped, banging his hand on the bar.

"Knew what?"

"I knew he was involved with that injun."

"In what way?"

"Selling guns, of course," he said.

"Wait a minute," I said, trying to control my excitement. "Are you saying that your partner was selling guns to the Indians?"

"I'm saying he must have been," he replied, "or else why would he have been out there?"

"Wait, wait," I said. "Hold it. Do you know for sure that he was selling guns?"

"Well, no, I don't know for sure. I always suspected it, but no, I can't swear to it."

"Would you tell your suspicions to the military?" I asked.

He shrugged and said, "If they asked me, why not?"

"That's great," I said, throwing a coin on the bar to pay for my beer.

"Wait a minute," he said, as I prepared to rush off. "Why are you so interested?"

"Right now, the military, in the person of your young Colonel Mackenzie, is under the impression that I have been selling guns to the Indians. Your suspicions concerning your partner, coupled with his being killed, might just be what I need to get me off the hook," I explained.

"Is that so?" he asked, raising his eyebrows. "Well then, good luck, friend."

"That's just what I'll need," I told him. "Luck . . . and you."

Chapter Eighteen

"Say that again?" I asked Mackenzie the following afternoon. That morning I had gone to his office to tell him about Jed Jordan's suspicions, and now it was afternoon, and he had sent for me. Then he had told me something I didn't believe—or didn't want to believe.

"Jed Jordan said that his partner would never have had the guts to sell guns to the Indians," Mackenzie repeated for me. "Now suppose you tell me what kind of game you're playing, Adams? Are you that nervous that you'd try to blame a dead man?"

"Hey, I'm not nervous, colonel," I corrected him. "I'm sick. I'm sick of Fort Sill, I'm sick of soldiers who rape little girls, and I'm sick of you."

He stood up so fast he knocked over his chair. I thought he was going to come around the desk at me—that is, I hoped he would. Instead he just stood there and said, "Adams, don't push me too far."

"Why? I might prejudice the investigation? Come on, Mackenzie, you've been after me ever since I sided with an Indian against your men, even if that Indian was a little girl."

"Little savage, you mean!" he replied tightly. "They're all savages, Adams, and Quanah is the biggest savage of all. If I find that you're the one—"

"I'm not the one, colonel," I said, cutting him off, "so you're going to have to find another way of getting me. Meanwhile, I'll get your man for you. You can bet on it."

I walked out without listening to his reply. It must not have been very important, because he let me go.

Jed Jordan lied to Mackenzie. Why? The answer seemed obvious. His partner either was or wasn't selling guns to Quanah, but either way, I figured Jed Jordan *was* selling guns. Maybe his partner was in on it, and maybe not, but my guess was that they were working together, or else why would Holt end up dead on the Staked Plains?

I wasn't all that sure it was Quanah or one of his braves that killed him, either.

No, I was sure now that Jed Jordan was selling guns to Quanah, and had probably killed his partner, either after a falling out, or simply because he got tired of sharing the profits.

All I had to do now was prove it.

Chapter Nineteen

I went back to Jed Jordan's place, ordered a beer from him and sat at one of the tables. My problem now was how to prove that he was the one selling guns to Quanah's Indians, not me. There were a couple of ways I could have tried it. One was to watch him, and hope that he led me to some guns.

The other possibility was to go to Dancing Fawn and let her bring me to Quanah Parker. Even if he wouldn't reveal who was selling the guns, he could at least tell someone that it wasn't me.

Tell someone—but who? I needed a witness that the military would accept. They certainly wouldn't believe Dancing Fawn, but who would they believe?

Two choices—and either one could get me killed. Which way to go? There were other things to take into consideration, also. If Jed Jordan was selling guns, he would probably stay away from it for a while, till things died down a bit after Holt's death. So if I sat and watched him for the next week or so, I'd get pretty bored, and get damned little done, and if Jordan figured out what I was up to, he'd get a good laugh out of it.

The way I figured it, then, I had about a week to try and get Quanah himself to help me.

That meant I'd accomplish more going to see Dancing

Fawn than sitting in Jordan's saloon in the middle of the day drinking beer. I got up, noticed Jordan watching me, nodded to him and left without receiving a nod in return.

I walked out the batwing doors, turned left and bounced off of Dutch Black.

"Jesus," I said, backing away from him a few steps. "Wear a bell, why don't you?"

"Huh?" he asked, frowning.

"Where's your leash?" I asked. "Teal lets you run around loose like that?"

"You tryin' to get me mad?" the big dummy asked me.

"No, you wouldn't want to go and do that without Joe Teal's say-so, would you, Dutch?" I asked him.

"I got a mind of my own," he declared.

"Do you?" I asked. "I tell you what, when you find it, let me know. I've never seen a pea brain up close."

I walked past him before he could decide whether or not he had been insulted.

I took the roundabout route to Dancing Fawn's teepee, and then wondered if I was supposed to knock on something before I entered. Luckily for me, Dancing Willow chose that moment to pop her head out from beneath the flap and when she saw me she smiled and beckoned me in.

"Hello, Clint," Dancing Fawn greeted me.

"Hello. I've come to talk to you about Quanah Parker."

Fawn said something to Willow in their own language, and the little one left.

"Please, sit," Fawn invited me. I did so and she said, "You wish to find Quanah?"

As I understood it, the whites were the only ones who called him Quanah Parker. His own people simply referred to him as Quanah.

"Yes," I answered.

"Your colonel, he did not accept the dead man as proof of your innocence?"

"He did not. I think I will need Quanah, if you still agree to take me to him."

"It was my idea," she reminded me, "and you agreed. Yes, I will still take you."

"Fawn, what will Quanah do when he sees me?"

"You think he will kill you?" she asked.

"From everything I've heard—"

"You have only heard the white man speak of Quanah," she said, interrupting me. "He will not kill you while you are with me. He will listen to me."

"Will he help me?"

"If I ask him to," she answered, "and if he can."

"Why?"

"I do not understand," she said, and I was afraid we were going to play the same scene we had the afternoon before.

"Why will Quanah help me if you ask him to? Are you his wife, Fawn?"

"I have not been so honored," she replied. "Quanah's entire family is dead," she went on to explain. "He and I are as brother and sister, though it is not by blood."

"I see."

"When would you like to go?" she asked.

"In the morning, after first light," I said.

"You will bring me a horse?"

"I will."

"I will be waiting for you."

It sounded very much like a dismissal and I stood up.

"We may be gone for more than a day," I said. "What about Dancing Willow?"

"My people will care for her," she assured me. "The soldiers might look for me, though."

I had already thought of that. If Mackenzie found out

that she was gone, and that I was gone, he might send some of his troops after us, thinking to catch me in a meeting with Quanah.

What he would actually be doing was sending me the witnesses I needed when Quanah cleared me.

Very cooperative of him, too.

Chapter Twenty

For want of something better to do with the rest of the day, I went back to the saloon and sat on Jordan for a while, just to see his reaction. He was there the whole time, until after dark, without a replacement. He didn't seem to be particularly put off by my presence, and he hardly looked at me when I got up to leave.

I walked back to my hotel rather unsteadily, just slightly drunk from all the beer I'd been drinking. It was early, though, and a good, long night's sleep would leave me in good shape for the trip the following morning.

When I entered my room I became immediately aware that I was not alone.

"How did you get up here without anyone seeing you?" I asked Sheila Mackenzie.

"I came up the back way," she said. She was lying on my bed, fully dressed. "I hope you don't mind."

"That depends," I replied.

"On what?"

"On what you want." She was, after all, the colonel's wife. Could he have sent her up here, or was that being overly suspicious? If I was going to go that far, why not question what had happened between us before? Had he engineered that? I didn't think so.

She got up off the bed, walked up to me and took hold of both of my elbows.

I allowed her hand to stay on my left elbow, but shook the one on my right elbow off, to free my gun hand. Old habits do die hard. She didn't seem to notice that I'd done it deliberately.

"I came to be with you again, Clint," she said. She stood on her toes and kissed me on the mouth, chewing lightly on my lower lip.

"Isn't that rather dangerous?" I asked, sliding my hands onto her waist.

"I don't care," she whispered, and our mouths met again in a longer kiss. Her hands began to work feverishly on the buttons of my shirt, and then I started working on her clothes.

I pushed her back to the bed and we both fell on top of it, naked.

"Oh, yes," she breathed when I touched my lips to her beautiful breasts. Her nipples were already hard when I took first one and then the other between my teeth.

"I couldn't wait for this," she said in a reverent tone. "I couldn't wait."

Her hands reached between us and took hold of me eagerly, and then I thrust myself inside of her as hard as I could.

She gripped my buttocks with surprising strength and I slid my hands beneath her and did the same. We ground ourselves together as if we were trying to crawl inside of each other's skin. Her breath was coming in short, choppy huffs as I plunged in and out of her, and then her breathing stopped and her body tensed in anticipation of her orgasm.

Afterward I asked her, "Won't your husband be looking for you?"

"If he comes home before I do, he'll see my bedroom door closed and assume I'm asleep."

"You have separate bedrooms?"

"Yes. Ronald had been chasing Quanah Parker for so

many years now that catching him is all he ever thinks about. That is his passion." Her tone of voice said she was resigned to that situation. Or at least, she was until she'd met me.

"He's a fool," I said.

"He's a sick man," she corrected me.

"Why don't you leave him?"

I hadn't turned up the lamp since entering the room, and in the darkness I could feel her shrug.

"I've got nowhere to go, Clint, and nobody to go with."

"Sheila—" I began, but she touched my mouth with her hand.

"I'm not asking you to take me with you, Clint, don't worry. I recognize this for what it is, and I accept it."

"Sheila—"

She rolled into my arms and said, "Don't say anything else, Clint, just make love to me again."

Her mouth was all hot and searching, and there was little I could do to resist it.

I didn't even want to try.

Chapter Twenty-One

I picked Dancing Fawn up nice and early the next day. I hadn't had as much sleep as I had anticipated, but I felt pretty good anyway.

Fawn rode without a saddle, and she rode very well, moving as though she were one with the animal. She kept her head up high and rode proudly. Many of the Indians I had seen on the reservation had started walking with their heads down, but not Dancing Fawn, and not her little sister, Dancing Willow. Maybe it was because she was almost a sister to the great chief, Quanah, or maybe she was just proud to be who she was.

When we reached the place where we had found Amos Holt, we stopped for a short rest.

"How much farther?" I asked.

"That depends on Quanah," she said. "If he sees us, he may follow us for a while before he lets us know."

"You mean he could be following us right now?" I asked.

"He, or one of his braves," she said.

"When will he let us know?"

"When he is ready."

After years as a lawman—dealing with every kind of person—I knew that with Indians it was best to follow their lead. Their strict code of honor usually let you know where you stood with them. In this case, under Dancing Fawn's protection, I figured I'd best do everything her way—or Quanah's way. When she started off again, I controlled the urge I had to look around, and followed.

The Staked Plains were barren and empty, dry and hard. It was a timberless tableland, bordered by steep escarpments. There could have been any number of Quanah's braves up there, and if any one of them had a particular dislike for white men, I could be wearing an arrow in my back at any moment. My back began to itch, but I kept my head straight ahead. Above all else, Indians respected courage and despised cowardice. At the first sign of weakness from me, I'd be wearing enough feathered shafts to resemble a peacock.

When darkness started to fall I said to Fawn, "I guess Quanah wants to see just how bad I want to find him."

"He may be testing you," she admitted. We had started a fire and were trying to keep warm. "Do you want to turn back in the morning?"

"No, we'll keep going," I said.

She smiled for one of the few times since we'd met and said, "That is good. Quanah will respect you for that."

"I think it's Quanah's feelings towards you that are going to count more than his feelings towards me," I commented.

"One can never tell what Quanah will decide, or why," she said, and that didn't fill me with a whole lot of confidence. Here we were sitting right in the middle of Quanah's own country, and now she was telling me how unpredictable he was.

"He'll listen to you, though," I said.

"He will listen," she agreed, "and then he will decide." She touched my hand and added, "You will be brave, Clint, and he will help you."

Sure, I thought, but which part was going to be the hardest, being brave face to face with the infamous Quanah Parker, or getting him to help me?

Chapter Twenty-Two

As it turned out, I didn't have to wait very long the next day for Quanah to make up his mind. Somebody kept nudging me until I woke up, and I found myself looking up into the painted face of an Indian brave. My first instinct was to go for my gun, but I quelled it and sat up. I looked around and saw Dancing Fawn and a half-dozen other braves.

"Are you all right?" I asked her.

"Yes. They will take us to Quanah. They want you to get up and saddle your horse."

"Okay, honey, whatever you say."

I saddled Duke and they watched, speaking among themselves and eyeing the big black with admiration.

"Easy, boy," I told Duke, patting his neck. "If we watch ourselves, we'll get out of this in one piece."

Duke gave me a look that might have been a bit dubious, but he usually went along with anything I said, and this time was no exception. He stood calmly while I saddled him, and then mounted. Fawn and the others had already mounted up and when I was ready she said, "This way."

We started out in a straight line, with me in the middle. The thing that surprised me was that Fawn was leading the way. I guessed that she must have known where Quanah was all along, she had just been waiting for him to send word that it was all right to bring me in.

My respect for her deepened the more I knew of her. Those six braves treated her like she was some kind of a princess, and when I thought about it, that was always the way she acted—like royalty.

It was probably on her word, too, that I still had my gun and rifle. Apparently, Quanah trusted her judgment, and it began to look better to me that he might help me if she asked him to.

We rode half a day before we finally reached our destination. I was the center of attraction as we rode into Quanah's camp. Finally, Fawn stopped and slid off her horse. We all stopped, and I didn't move until she reached me.

"You can step down off your horse, Clint," she said. I did so and she called a brave over and told me, "Give him the reins. He will take good care of your horse."

Duke whinnied nervously, but I spoke softly to him and handed the brave his reins.

"Tell him not to try and touch his head," I instructed Fawn, "or he'll lose his hand."

She spoke to the brave and he looked at me, and then at Duke, then gingerly led the big boy away.

"Where's Quanah?" I asked her.

"He will come," she said. "You must be patient. I will take you somewhere so you can wait."

She walked off and I followed her, surprised that none of the braves came with us. Apparently, I was free to walk about the camp, even with my gun, as long as I was with Fawn.

"Wait in here," she said, pulling aside the flap of a teepee.

I waited for her to say something else, but when she didn't I stepped inside and she let the flap fall closed behind me.

Okay, so here I was, right in the middle of Quanah's camp, waiting for the big man to grant me an audience. Either that or have me killed.

Isn't it funny how after you've gotten into something with both feet, you wonder if it was a good idea after all?

Chapter Twenty-Three

They kept me waiting almost an hour, which I felt was still part of Quanah's test of me, which had begun when we were traveling on the Plains. I wondered if the test would be over when I finally met him, or if it would be just beginning.

I heard voices outside the teepee and then the flap was drawn back. As I stood up, Dancing Fawn walked in first—followed by Quanah.

He was a tall, striking looking man in his thirties. His body was sinewy and hard, his hair lighter than I would have expected on an Indian. The two features that stood out the most, however, were the fact that he was wearing a sidearm in a holster, and that his eyes were blue. I reminded myself that the great chief Quanah was only half Indian—and half white.

He stepped in and stood with his arms at his sides, studying me critically. I met his gaze and held it, determined not to look away. He was wearing black war paint in such a way that he looked like Satan himself.

"You are Adams?" he finally asked.

"I am."

"I am Quanah."

"I am honored that you would see me," I said.

"It is because you helped Dancing Fawn, and her sister, Dancing Willow, that I have agreed to see you," he said, making sure I knew that it wasn't because he loved me like a brother.

"I am aware of that," I replied, "and I am grateful to you for seeing me, no matter what the reason."

He looked at Fawn and said, "Leave us," in a tone that left no room for argument.

When she left, he looked at me and, in the same tone, said, "Sit."

I sat, and so did he.

"Has Dancing Fawn explained my problem to you?" I asked.

"Dancing Fawn has told me that she wants me to help you, because you helped her," he replied. "You will tell me what your problem is."

I was impressed by his near-perfect English.

"Well, then, my problem is guns."

"Guns?"

"And the fact that someone is selling them to you," I elaborated.

His blue eyes became much colder than they already were—if that was possible—and he folded his arms across his chest and stared at me in silence.

"Continue," he said, finally.

"It seems that the military—"

"Colonel Mackenzie?" he asked.

"Yes. It seems the colonel has it in his mind that I might be the one selling you the guns. He has taken my property and is holding it while he investigated."

"Why does he think you are selling guns?"

"I don't think he does, really. He would like to blame me for something, just because I helped Dancing Willow escape from his three soldiers."

He regarded me in silence again, then said, "I understand. The colonel is no friend of yours, just as he is no friend of mine."

"Exactly."

"If I help you, I would be causing him some difficulty," he commented.

I was glad that he was looking at it that way. "You would."

He nodded and continued to examine me.

"If I tell you who is selling me the guns, you will tell him. Correct?"

"I would have to," I admitted, which may have been foolish, "in order to clear myself."

"And then I would get no more guns," he finished.

"I'm afraid that is what it would amount to," I agreed.

"Then you see that you are not the only one with a problem," he said. "If I help you, I do not help my people."

"There is another way," I said.

His face remained impassive, but he asked, "How?"

"All you would have to do is tell them that it isn't me who is selling you the guns," I said.

"Would Colonel Mackenzie take my word?" he asked.

He had me stumped, there. Mackenzie would just believe that Quanah was trying to protect his source of weapons, wouldn't he? Why should he believe the very man he's been trying to catch, or kill, for the past couple of years?

"You will stay the night," Quanah said, rising, "here. Do not attempt to walk through the camp without Dancing Fawn, or someone who I have sent. There are many of my braves who would like to torture you to death."

"Nice of them to want to make me feel welcome," I remarked, but it went right past him.

"We will both think about our problems over night, and in the morning we will come to a decision."

"One that will help both of us, I hope."

"One that will satisfy my debt to you," he said, and I figured that would have to do me until morning.

Chapter Twenty-Four

I spent the night in that teepee alone. I didn't see Quanah, Dancing Fawn, or anyone again until first light, and I slept surprisingly well, considering where I was.

Quanah's braves showed admirable restraint allowing me to make it until morning without being the least bit tortured. The first person I saw was Fawn, who brought me something to eat.

"What is it?" I asked, looking into the bowl. It was some kind of pasty substance, which seemed to have chunks of meat in it. A spoon had been fashioned from a tree branch, and I used it to shovel the gruel into my mouth.

"Is it good?" she asked.

"It is," I said, surprised.

"Then I will not tell you what it is."

I stopped eating for a moment, but my stomach complained, and I allowed the matter of what I was eating pass, and got back to eating it.

"Have you spoken to Quanah?" I asked.

"Yes, but not about you. When he has made a decision, he will tell you, not me."

"But it's your debt he's paying, isn't it?"

She shook her head.

"The debt is his now," she said, and did not elaborate.

She got up to leave and I said, "Won't you eat with me?"

"I must cook with the other women," she said. "When the warriors have eaten, then we will eat."

"I'll see you later, then."

"Yes," she said, and left.

When morning became afternoon, I started to wonder how long Quanah was going to make me wait. Was he still testing my nerve?

As if to answer that question, the flap to my teepee opened, and three braves stepped in, all decked out in war paint, followed by Quanah.

The four of them stood there staring at me and I didn't know exactly what I was supposed to do, so I picked out Quanah's blue eyes and stared at them.

"My people want to kill you, Clint Adams," Quanah finally said.

"Well," I said, "that's no way to pay a debt."

"The debt is mine, not theirs. If I tell you who is selling us the guns, my people will pay the price."

"I'm sure you have plenty of guns, Quanah," I remarked.

"Guns no good without bullets," one of the other braves spoke up.

I stared at him, and then back at Quanah and asked, "You have no bullets for the guns?"

"We have bullets, but not enough," Quanah said. "So you see, if I pay you the debt, my people also pay it."

"We not want to pay," the other brave said. "We kill you, instead."

"Somehow," I said to Quanah, "this isn't my idea of a solution that suits us both."

"There is another way," he said.

"And what's that?"

"If you could prove that you are worthy of the sacrifice my people would have to make, then I can help you."

"And how do I do that?" I asked suspiciously.

"You must prove your courage and strength."

"Against who . . . or what?" I asked.

"Against these three braves," he said, indicating the three men with him.

"How do we do that?" I asked. "Do I have to fight the three of them at one time? Is that how you test honor?"

"We are not testing your honor," Quanah said, "but your courage, your strength and your ability."

"Ability to do what?"

They all looked at each other, and then Quanah said, "To stay alive."

I looked at the three Indians and they looked as if, individually, they would be very formidable.

"What weapons?" I asked.

"No weapons," the other brave spoke up. The remaining two braves never spoke, and I never did learn if it was because they couldn't speak English, or just didn't want to.

"How do we do this?" I asked again.

"A few miles from here there is a box canyon," he said. "You will have a head start, on foot, and they will follow soon after. You will walk to the canyon and go inside. Once you see them enter, you must try to get out and return here, unharmed."

"Totally unharmed?" I asked.

"You must have received no serious physical injury," he amended.

"If I receive a serious injury," I said, "I'll never make it back anyway."

He simply looked at me and nodded, his face as immobile as stone.

Chapter Twenty-Five

They fed me well that night, like an animal who was to be slaughtered the next day. My food was served to me in my teepee by Dancing Fawn, who this time stayed with me while I ate.

"You're not going to tell me what this is either, are you?" I asked her, as I bit into a piece of plump, juicy meat.

"Is it good?" she asked again.

I laughed and said, "Yes, it's very good."

"Then why ruin it by asking what it is?" she answered, in all seriousness.

"You're right."

We ate together, and she was strangely silent. Not that her being silent was strange, but there was something else underneath this particular silence.

"You have troubles?" I asked her, using the same words she'd used on me once.

"Yes," she said without lifting her head, "I have troubles." She looked at me and said, "I do not like the thought that I brought you here and now you may die."

"Well, to tell you the truth," I replied, "I don't like the thought either, so why don't we both just not think about it, okay?"

"I cannot help but think about it," she said.

"Dancing Fawn," I said, putting down the food she'd brought me, "do you want to help me?"

"You know I do."

"Then don't think about it, and help me not to think about it, all right?"

She lifted her eyes from the ground again and looked at me very solemnly. "I will stay with you," she said.

"Wait a minute," I said, "I didn't mean—"

"You do not want me to stay?" she asked.

"No—I mean, that's not it at all—" I stammered. She was the only woman in recent memory who had caused me to stammer.

"Then I will stay," she said. There was a small fire in the center of the teepee, and she rose and dropped the deerskin dress she was wearing, causing the firelight to flicker on her smooth, sun-burnished skin. I had glimpsed her once before, briefly, and this time I took a much better look. Her breasts were incredibly full and round, with large, brown nipples. The firelight caused shaded valleys between her breasts and thighs, valleys that I wanted very much to explore.

I lay back on a blanket that had been spread for me, and she lay beside me.

"Do Indians kiss?" I asked.

"Kiss?" she asked. She touched her fingers to my mouth and said, "Is this what you call the touching of the lips?"

"Yes, that's it," I said, smiling.

She traced her fingers over my lips and said, "I have seen this done, but have never experienced it. May we try now?"

"My pleasure," I said.

I pulled her face down to me and first kissed her high cheekbones before touching my mouth to hers. She kept her lips tight and I broke the contact after a few seconds.

"You must relax, Fawn," I told her. I kissed her then,

and the tightness was gone from her lips. They were soft and full, and when I kissed her a third time, she kissed me back and asked for more.

After a few minutes she had it right, and I moved on to other things. I began to circle her nipples with my tongue as she poised herself over me, dangling her full breasts in my face. As I bit her nipples she smiled, transforming her face from lovely to absolutely beautiful.

I worked my clothes off, and she pressed her body down along the length of mine. Her flesh was very hot, and her nipples were hard as they scraped my chest. I flipped her over so that she was lying on her back, and then I explored her entire body with my tongue and lips, enjoying very much my first taste of an Indian girl, and this Indian girl in particular.

When I entered her, she tightened her arms around me and sank her teeth into my shoulder to smother her cries of pleasure and passion. As I continued to stroke her, she became more active, running her hands over me, wrapping her legs around me, and moving her hips in time with mine.

We were kissing when she came the first time, and she bit my tongue painfully, but I didn't mind, because my own orgasm was building, and when she finally came for the second time, I exploded inside of her.

After that she smiled a lot more and we talked about a lot of things, and tried out her kissing some more. We never talked about what the morning would bring, but I knew we were both thinking about it.

I had to beat three Indians at their own game just to get Quanah to speak for me, and then there was still no guarantee that it would even help.

Chapter Twenty-Six

When I woke the next morning, Dancing Fawn had already gone. I assumed that Quanah knew that she had intended to stay the night with me, and hadn't objected, but I still felt better that she wasn't there when he came to get me.

"You are ready?" he asked, as he stepped into my teepee.

"As ready as I'll ever be," I replied.

"You are in good spirits. That is good."

"Yeah, it's just great."

He surprised me by clapping me on the shoulder and saying, "You are a brave man, Clint Adams. You will succeed."

"Your braves are also brave men, Quanah, are they not?" I asked.

"They are very brave," he said. "Come, it is time."

As I started to follow he turned and said, "Leave your weapon."

I unbuckled my gunbelt and laid it down, then followed him out.

The entire village seemed to have turned out to see the white man go against three of their own. Dancing Fawn was standing with the women, and when she looked at me it was without expression. I decided that, since she didn't look worried, I would take that as a vote of confidence.

"Stand over here," Quanah said, beckoning me to stand beside him. The three braves I was supposed to evade were standing off to one side, talking among themselves.

As I took up position beside Quanah he said to me, "Take off your boots."

"What?" I asked, staring at him. Was I expected to run all the way to that boxed canyon and back in my bare feet?

Actually, from the look on most of the faces around me, I wasn't even expected to make it to the canyon, and without boots they might have been right.

"My boots," I repeated.

He nodded, and I proceeded to do as he said. When I had them off a child came over and took them from me, and then handed me a pair of moccasins. I breathed a sigh of relief and gratefully accepted them from him. They were very thin, but at least I'd be wearing the same footwear as my opposition.

When I had them fit snugly onto my feet I stood up straight and looked at Quanah expectantly.

"Do you see that peak?" he asked.

I looked where he was pointing and said, "Yes." Jesus, I hoped that wasn't where I was supposed to run to. That was miles away.

"If you keep moving towards that peak, you will soon come to the canyon my people call the Canyon of Death."

"That's a catchy name," I commented.

"You start now," he instructed me. "You will have a mile head start, and then I will start my braves. I warn you, they will try to catch you before you reach the canyon, and they are very fast runners."

I looked at the three of them, all tall, thin and long-legged and didn't doubt it.

"Start, Clint Adams, and luck to you," Quanah said.

I looked over at Dancing Fawn, who kept her face expressionless, and then started off at a trot.

I could feel every pebble and rock through the moccasins, but at least they kept my feet from getting cut to pieces. I alternated running and walking until I judged that I had gone a mile, then I tried to run or trot most of the time. My lungs started to burn, but I kept up as steady a pace as I could manage and thought about what would happen once I reached that box canyon.

It had to figure that those three braves would be in much better shape than I was when they reached it. Horses had been doing most of my running for years, a fact that was already beginning to tell on my legs. Once I was in that canyon, and they also entered, how the hell was I going to get out? Not only that, but I had it in my mind to get out without killing them. I wasn't afraid to face them, one at a time or all together, but it would be much easier if I could avoid them and get back to Quanah's camp.

After another fifteen minutes or so under the sun, I thought about taking off my shirt, but all that would do would be to get me burned to a crisp. When I got so thirsty it hurt, I started thinking about other things, to keep my mind off of it. As the perspiration began to drip off my nose I caught it with my tongue. It was salty, but at least it was wet.

It had been a couple of hours after first light when Quanah had finally started me, so I knew that the sun would still be high when I reached the canyon. I was going to have to find some other way than the cover of darkness to slip out after my adversaries entered. Maybe there'd be some kind of a crevice I could hide in right by the mouth, and after they passed I could start back to the camp while they searched the canyon for me.

I kept thinking about finding different ways in and out of that canyon, forgetting about my thirst and the fact that my feet hurt, until I finally reached it.

It was a small canyon, and just inside the mouth I found a small path to the top. I used the path to get up high and look behind me. Sure enough, those three braves were fast runners. I could make out their figures and they were moving fast, seemingly tireless. I figured I had less than fifteen minutes before they reached me, fifteen minutes to figure a way out of that canyon.

I sat at the top of that path, catching my breath and looking the canyon over. From where I sat, I could see most of it, and there was no other obvious way in or out besides the way I'd entered.

And then it struck me. I had only gone a few feet into the canyon before encountering the small trail. Maybe they'd walk by the trail and go all the way in, and then I'd be able to slip past them. If not, if they saw the trail, it was too small for the three of them to come at me at once. They'd have to approach me one at a time, and that was fine by me.

I decided that right where I sat was the best place to be, and I watched as the braves rapidly closed the distance between us.

I hoped I'd be able to return to the camp without killing any of them. I didn't know how strongly Quanah felt about his "debt" to me, and whether or not it would survive my killing some of his men.

How would his people feel about his debt, then?

Chapter Twenty-Seven

When they got close enough for me to see the paint of their faces, I withdrew as far as I could, so as not to be seen.

When they reached the mouth of the canyon they stopped and talked, apparently mapping out their strategy. When they'd decided how they were going to work it, two of them went into the canyon, and one stayed at the entrance. Obviously, he was going to wait there in case I doubled back. That suited me, too. I'd only have to deal with him in order to start back.

I gave the other two a good head start, so that they wouldn't be able to hear anything that went on between the third one and me.

I recognized the third man right away. He was the brave who had spoken English inside the teepee, the one who had kept looking at me like he wanted to carve me up right then and there. I wondered if he just hated me, or hated me as a representative of all white men. Or could it have even been something else?

Like Dancing Fawn?

I took a few moments to decide how to take him. If I tried to scramble down that path at him he'd become alerted, maybe yell for the others. The best thing to do would be to try and get him to come up after me.

He stood at the mouth of that canyon with his arms crossed, waiting for me to come out of it, or for his brothers to come out carrying my body.

I got up on my heels and rolled a few pebbles down that small path. The brave looked up briefly, but then turned his head back to the canyon. I picked up some larger stones and rolled them down. This time he looked up with interest. He unfolded his arms and walked towards the sound, and I could tell by the look on his face that he'd spotted the small trail. He looked around, and then decided to go ahead and climb it.

As he approached the top I moved out into view and the surprise was plain on his face. I didn't give him a chance to recover from it. I threw myself at him, and we went tumbling down that trail together.

I was ready for the fall and he wasn't, so I was the first to recover. I set myself and waited for him to scramble to his feet, and then I swung a right that caught him high on the cheekbone. As he staggered back I followed and threw a punch into his belly. He doubled over, but he was quick. He ran forward and buried his head in my stomach. We were both off balance and went stumbling to the ground. We rolled about on the hard ground and I could feel the sharp rocks cutting me up some. We broke apart and I scrambled to my feet, but he had gotten to his first. He threw a kick that landed on my side and would have done more damage if he'd been wearing boots instead of moccasins. I rolled with it and came back to my feet as he charged me. I sidestepped and stuck my foot out, tripping him, and then hit him behind the ear as he went down. He hit the ground on his face and didn't move. I nudged him with my foot, just in case he was playing possum, but he was unconscious.

I checked the canyon, but there was no sign of the other two braves. I rolled the unconscious Indian behind some brush, left him there and started back for the camp. As long as the other two didn't find him too soon, I was home free. That would make the trip back a little easier than the trip there or so I hoped.

As dusk fell, I was wondering who would be waiting to see which of us would get back first. I also started to wonder if I had gone in the right direction. I felt sure I should have reached the camp already. What a laugh if I had successfully eluded Quanah's warriors only to get lost and die—

Suddenly, I spotted what I thought were some fires, and as I got closer I could see that I had finally reached the camp.

There were only two people waiting there now: Quanah and Dancing Fawn. They were in virtually the same positions they had been in when I left. It was as if all of the others had gone, and those two had never moved during the whole day.

When Fawn saw me, she stood up and walked over to stand beside Quanah. I slowed my pace entering the camp and stopped directly in front of them.

"Clint," Fawn said softly. Her voice betrayed the tension she must have been feeling the entire day, that she must have been feeling even that morning, though she hadn't let it show on her face.

Quanah didn't say anything, he just ran his eyes over me very deliberately, obviously inspecting me for injury.

"Are you all right?" Dancing Fawn asked me.

I nodded, because I wasn't yet able to speak.

"You have done well," Quanah finally said. "Have you killed my men?"

I swallowed, caught my breath, and said, "Your men are fine, Quanah. None of them is seriously hurt."

He looked surprised, which was the first change of expression I had seen on him since I'd met him.

"I am impressed," he said. "You have won, and I will honor my debt to you."

"Thank you," I said, still panting, "but if it's all the same to you, right now all I'd like is a drink of water."

Chapter Twenty-Eight

They gave me water, food and rest and the next morning the only reminders of the previous day's ordeal were the blisters on my feet and the sun blisters on the back of my neck.

Dancing Fawn woke me that morning and said that she had come to bathe my feet and neck, which she did, and then she put on some kind of salve that she said would take care of the blisters.

"I will bring you something to eat," she said afterward, "and then Quanah will come to speak to you."

"Good," I said, "thank you."

"I am very pleased and proud that you are all right," she said as she got up to leave.

"Have the other three returned?"

"Yes, during the night. They spoke angrily with Quanah, but he will not listen to their words."

"They must be embarrassed," I said.

"I must go now," she said. "Quanah will come soon."

"Thank you, Dancing Fawn, for everything," I said.

She gave me a fleeting smile and then left.

I lay back and waited for the ache in my feet and neck to subside, and surprisingly it did, rather quickly, thanks once again to Dancing Fawn. I owed her a lot.

A little while later Quanah came in and sat down

wordlessly. He still seemed to have a great deal on his mind, and I didn't say anything, letting him speak at his own pace.

"I have decided," he said, finally.

"What is your decision?" I asked him.

"I have decided to go back to the fort with you."

"What?" I asked, not believing what I'd heard him say.

"I will go back with you and tell them that you are not selling guns to my people. Perhaps they will believe me if I do this."

His point was valid, but he didn't realize who he was dealing with. In all this time, hadn't it occurred to him that Colonel Mackenzie was not an honorable man? Did he really think that Mackenzie would let him leave the fort once he was inside?

"I appreciate your gesture, Quanah, but—"

"I have decided," he said firmly, rising. "We will leave when you are able to travel."

I stood up and said, "I can travel now, but I want you to understand what might happen—"

"I will pay my debt to you in this way, Clint Adams," he said. "That is my decision."

He turned and went out through the flap of the teepee and I stood there, flabbergasted. How could he just walk into Mackenzie's hands like that? And what was I going to do about it? What could I do about it? Quanah was a great chief, and he had made his decision. The only thing I could possibly do was try to keep him alive inside the fort, and try to make sure he got out in one piece again.

Very soon after Dancing Fawn came back in and said, "Your horse is ready."

I nodded, got up and followed her out. There were three horses ready. Apparently Dancing Fawn was coming back with us, also.

"Why don't you stay, Fawn?" I asked her.

"My people need me," she said very simply.

"Savages" my people called them, but I had seen more white savages than red ones in the past week or so, and now I was bringing Quanah Parker right into their hands.

Chapter Twenty-Nine

Quanah's reception as he rode through the reservation was impressive. At first a murmuring ran throughout his captured people, but then they all fell silent and just watched as he rode among them like a god.

Inside the fort, it was quite different. There were soldiers running back and forth, holding their guns on him, and he took absolutely no notice of them at all. I turned a few times to make sure he was still there and had not been dragged off his horse by the white savages in blue uniforms. By the time I stopped in front of Mackenzie's office, there was a sea of blue surrounding us. I dismounted and Quanah followed. I signaled Dancing Fawn to dismount also, because I feared what would happen to her if we left her outside.

When we walked into Mackenzie's outer office, his sergeant sprang to his feet at the sight of Quanah and grabbed for his gun.

"At ease, sergeant," I said, holding up my hand. "Tell the colonel that I'm here and I have brought a guest."

"An Indian?" he asked incredulously.

"Not just an Indian," I said. "Tell him that Quanah is here."

He backed his way to the colonel's door, obviously

afraid to turn his back for fear of catching an arrow in it. He grabbed for the knob and slipped into the room, shutting the door behind him.

Moments later he reappeared at the heels of Colonel Ronald Mackenzie.

"By God, it's true," Mackenzie said when he saw us. "You've captured Quanah! Adams, if you wanted to clear yourself, you sure as hell picked the right way to do it."

Some soldiers had crowded into the room behind us, including Joe Teal and his crew, and to Mackenzie I said, "Could we go into your office, colonel?"

"By all means," he said.

"Alone, colonel," I added. "Just you, me, Quanah and the girl."

He looked dubious, but agreed.

In his office he sat behind his desk and regarded Quanah, who stared back stoically. This might have been the first time the two enemies had come face to face during all the time they'd been fighting each other.

"How did you capture him?" he demanded.

"I didn't," I answered. "Quanah is here of his own free will, colonel, to clear me of the charge of selling guns to the Indians."

He stared at me and said, "You're joking."

"No, I'm not. He agreed to come in and speak to you on my behalf, and I guaranteed that he would be able to walk out the same way he came in."

"You're mad," Mackenzie told me, "absolutely mad, Adams, if you think I'm going to let this—this savage walk out of this fort. And as for his clearing you, how could you expect me to take his word that you are not selling him guns? The man would obviously be protecting his source of weapons with such a statement."

He stood up behind his desk and leaned forward, placing his palms flat on the desk top and resting his weight on them.

"I'll tell you what I'll do, though. Since you've delivered him to me, I'll drop the investigation, release your property, and you can be on your way."

I shook my head. "That's not the way we're going to play it, colonel. Quanah came here to make a statement. He's going to make it, and then he's going to walk out of here, mount his horse and ride out."

"Not a chance," Mackenzie said, but I ignored him. I turned to Quanah and said, "Tell him."

"Clint Adams is not the man who has been selling my people guns," Quanah said without inflection.

"Oh?" Mackenzie asked. "If that's the case, then who has?"

"That *would* be giving away his source, colonel. Quanah came into this fort because he felt his word would carry more weight if he did it this way. Why else would he come here willingly?"

"To protect you against arrest, which would deprive him of any further assistance from you," Mackenzie said. "But my offer still stands, Adams. Ride out, and leave this savage to me."

I looked at Quanah and said, "I am sorry, Quanah. He is without honor, as you can see."

Quanah looked at me and nodded, but did not speak.

Mackenzie went red in the face at my words, and then called out, "Sergeant!"

The sergeant came rushing in, Joe Teal at his heels.

"Arrest these men!" Mackenzie instructed them, and I moved before I even had time to think about it.

I drew my gun, pointed it at the colonel, and cocked it. He looked shocked first, and then angry.

"You're crazy," he told me.

"This man is going to ride out of this fort unharmed," I said to him tightly.

"Then you had better go with him, Adams, because if he does, you're as good as dead. I'll have you hung—"

"I'll go one step further," I broke in. "I'll go with

him, and you'll go with us. Let's go."

I heard some movement behind me and said, "If anyone tries to interfere, colonel, I'll blow your head off."

He believed me, I knew, because it showed on his face. He looked past me at his men and said, "Don't try anything." He addressed himself to me again and said, "How far do you think you'll get, Adams?"

"I'll worry about that later. Right now my main concern is to get Quanah out of here."

"But he's the enemy, man!" he snapped. "Don't you understand? If we keep him here, we'll have won."

"I gave him my word," I said.

"This is treason—"

"Let's move, colonel."

He picked up his hat and started to reach for his gunbelt.

"You won't need that," I said, and his hand stopped inches away from the weapon.

"Teal," I called out behind me, "are you there?"

"I'm here, Adams," his voice answered, "waiting for a chance at your—"

"Get your boss a horse, and have a path cleared to the gate. If anyone tries anything, Teal, I'll kill him. Remember that, and make sure they know it outside."

He had obviously looked to Mackenzie for confirmation, because I saw the colonel nod and heard Teal leave the room.

We stood like that for as long as it took Teal to comply with my instructions, and then he came back and said, "The horse is ready."

"Good," I said. "Now clear out. I don't want anyone in that outer office, and I want to be able to see everyone's hands when we come out into the compound."

Again Mackenzie had to nod before Teal obeyed.

"Okay, colonel, let's go," I said. "You're going out

ahead of us. Get on your horse and wait for my word. Don't even think about running, because I won't miss."

"I won't take a chance with my life, Adams," he assured me, "because I want to make sure I'm there to see you hang."

"Fine, then this will be easy," I answered.

The outer office was empty, and when we got outside all I could see was blue uniforms forming a path to the door.

"Tell them to make that path wider, Colonel," I instructed him. "I don't want my gun going off because some eager beaver felt I was too close not to grab."

He gave the order and we waited until his men backed away from each other, leaving us a nice, wide path.

"Okay, mount up," I said. Mackenzie got up on his horse, followed by Quanah and Dancing Fawn, both of whom had been very silent through the whole thing. I mounted up last, and then told Mackenzie, "Head for the gate."

Mackenzie preceded us, and Quanah, Fawn and I rode three abreast, with me in the middle. The soldiers mumbled and stared, but nobody made a move lest their beloved commander get his head blown off.

As we got to the gate, Mackenzie ordered it opened, and his men complied. As we rode through the reservation, it was the Indians' turn to stare at Mackenzie, who kept his back ramrod straight and his head high.

As we cleared the reservation, Mackenzie turned and looked at me, but I just motioned with my gun for him to keep on going. It was only when we had a couple of miles between us and the fort that I told him he could stop.

"Now what?" he asked.

"Now you stay here and we go on," I said. "Don't ride back until you feel you're out of range of my gun, colonel. If you start back too soon, I'll pick you off. It's up to you when you think you're safe enough, but I have to tell you that I rarely miss."

"I'm aware of your reputation, Adams," he said, shifting in his saddle uncomfortably.

"Good. I'll be seeing you, colonel."

"And I'll be seeing you, as well, Adams—at the end of a rope," he advised me.

I gave him a smile I didn't feel, and then we rode on while he stood there and tried to gauge when I would be out of range. I turned back when I knew I was out of range, but he was still sitting there, waiting. Obviously, he wasn't taking any chances. After that, I didn't look back again.

Chapter Thirty

We rode a few more miles, and then we stopped.

"What will you do now?" Quanah asked. "You cannot return to your own people."

"I know, and I can't very well go with you. I would never be accepted by yours. I'll have to go back."

"You cannot," Dancing Fawn said. "They will kill you. Quanah," she went on, looking at her chief, "he saved your life."

Quanah looked at me and said, "That is true. Once again I am in your debt."

"That is not necessary," I assured him. "You tried to help me and it didn't work, but I'm very grateful."

"I am once again in your debt," Quanah insisted, "and I must pay."

"Really—" I started, but his next words startled me into silence.

"Jed Jordan," he said.

"What?"

"That is the name of the man who has been selling guns to my people," he answered. "Jed Jordan."

I digested that for a moment, and then asked. "What about his partner? His friend?"

"A fat man with no courage?" he asked.

"That's him."

"I can only assume that he killed him. When last we met, Jordan asked me for an arrow."

"Which he stuck in his partner's belly, so you and your people would be blamed for killing him."

"Jordan is also without honor," Quanah said, "and I would not deal with him if I did not have to."

"But why are you telling me this now?" I asked. "If I can convince the military that it's been Jordan selling guns and not me, that will cut off your supply."

Quanah shrugged. "The debt must be paid . . . and if Jordan is stopped, another will take his place."

That was very true. There would always be someone else looking to make a profit, no matter how many lives it cost.

"We are even now, Quanah," I said.

"Yes. There are no other debts between us," he said.

"What about Dancing Fawn? Mackenzie is not going to forget that she was also there."

"She will come back with me."

"I cannot," she cried. "What of Dancing Willow? What of my sister?"

"Is she safe now?" I asked.

"She is being cared for."

"I'll try and figure a way of getting her out," I promised, "with no debt owed in return." I looked at Quanah and said, "I will do this because I have a debt to Dancing Fawn, for taking me to you. Agreed?"

He thought about it, then nodded and said, "Agreed."

"Whether I am able to clear myself or not," I said, "I will bring her to the Staked Plains. Your braves can take her from me there—and, I hope, they will not kill me."

"If you come to the Plains alone," Quanah said, "you will be slain as an enemy. If you come with Dancing Willow, you will be allowed to leave alive—but do not come back. I warn you!"

"I understand."

"Goodbye, Clint," Dancing Fawn said with moist eyes.

"Goodbye, Dancing Fawn."

"Come," Quanah said to her. He turned his horse and started off for the Staked Plains, to continue his war. Dancing Fawn looked back at me once, and then I turned my horse and started back. But where could I go? If I went to my hotel they'd be sure to grab me, but I had to get back into town. I had to prove that Jed Jordan was the one selling guns, as I had suspected.

I was back to where I started from before seeing Quanah. I still had to prove that Jordan was guilty, only this time I had no freedom of movement.

I was worse off than before.

Chapter Thirty-One

I was only able to think of one place I could go to for help, and even going there was taking a big chance, but what choice did I really have?

I circled around and approached the town from behind, from the east. I stopped when I came within sight of the homes that were spread out behind the town, trying to find the one I wanted. When I had it spotted I dismounted and left Duke behind some trees, where he would be well hidden.

"Be patient, big boy," I told him. "I'll be back as soon as I can."

He gave a low whinny that was almost a rumble, and I patted his neck and started off on foot.

When I reached the house I looked in the windows, hoping Mackenzie wasn't there. Chances were good that he was back in his office, organizing some kind of a search for me. Once I was fairly sure that Sheila Mackenzie was in the house alone I knocked on her back door.

Her face lit up at the sight of me, and then she looked worried and grabbed my elbow.

"Come inside, quickly, before someone sees you," she said, pulling me inside. She shut the door behind me, then came into my arms eagerly. I kissed her once, then held her at arm's length.

"I'm in trouble, Sheila," I said.

"What's wrong?"

"Has your husband been home today?"

She snorted and said, "He hasn't been home since yesterday, and I couldn't care if he never came home."

"Can I have a drink?"

"Of course. Come into the sitting room."

I followed her and waited while she poured me a whiskey and handed it to me. I drank half of it, and then we sat down together while I told her what happened.

"I wish I could have seen that," she said when I finished. "Ronald must have been mortified."

"Well he wasn't happy with me, I can tell you that much," I assured her.

"What can I do to help?" she asked, just as I had been hoping she would.

"I can't go back into town," I explained. "Can you go in and ask the man at the livery, Freddie, to meet me?"

"Here?"

"No, not here. That's too dangerous, for me and for you. Behind here there's a spray of trees. I'll be waiting there for him. Ask him to meet me there as soon as he can."

"Won't he turn you in?"

I shook my head.

"I don't think so. He's not too fond of authority, and he'll probably see it as a chance to make a few dollars."

"All right," she said, rising. "I'll change and go into town now."

"You'll have to buy something, make it look like you're going shopping."

"Well, that shouldn't be too hard," she said, smiling.

I pulled her to me and kissed her long and hard, so that when I let her go she was out of breath.

"Later," I said.

"Yes," she replied, breathlessly.

"You had better change."

"Yes," she said, the same way, then she shook her head and said, "Oh, of course. Would you like something to eat? There's some chicken in the kitchen. Take what you want."

While she went and changed I went into the kitchen and took some chicken legs, a few pieces of fruit, and some bread. I was tempted to take a bottle of whiskey, but Mackenzie might have noticed that missing. I put everything into a sack I found, and then walked to her bedroom door.

"Sheila?"

"I'm almost ready," she called out.

I knew that was a lie. She was the kind of woman who would take an hour to get ready, no matter what the reason. I couldn't wait.

"I'm leaving. I'll try and keep in contact with you, all right?"

"Yes, all right," she called. I heard her footsteps and then she stuck her head out the door. "Clint, be very careful. You humiliated Ronald, and he'll never forget that."

"I'll be careful," I promised. I kissed her shortly and left the way I came.

Chapter Thirty-Two

I went back to where Duke was grazing and sat down to my own feast. I was dog tired from riding all day, and had no idea how long it would take Sheila to give Freddie the message, and Freddie to respond, so I decided to go to sleep. I was confident that if anyone approached, Duke would sense it and wake me up.

I had a dreamless sleep and was awakened by Duke striking the ground with his hooves. I quickly got to my feet and put my hand on my gun, waiting for whoever was coming to show their face.

It was Freddie, and I relaxed as he came into my small hideaway.

"Man, you have gotten yourself into a lot of trouble, ain't you?" he asked.

"Looks like it."

He handed me a bottle of whiskey and said, "I thought you might be needin' this 'bout now."

"Thanks," I said, accepting it, "but what I need even more is a place to stay while I work this all out."

"You find out who's sellin' the guns?" he asked.

"I did," I replied, and then I hesitated, wondering just how much I should trust him.

"If you wasn't gonna trust me," he spoke up, "you wouldn't of sent me a message to meet you here—and what a messenger!" he added, widening his eyes in the darkness. "How did you work that?"

"Never mind. You're right, though. I guess I'll have to trust you. Jed Jordan's been selling the guns."

"Well now, that don't surprise me, none," he said. "That man'll do anything to turn a profit. You got to prove it now, though, ain't you?"

"I sure as hell do," I answered, "and I can't do it from out here. I've got to get into town."

"That won't be so hard," he said. "I'll pick you up tomorrow with my wagon and take you to the stable. You can stay there."

"What about Duke?"

"I can take him back with me tonight. Ain't nobody watching me. I'll take him the back way."

I thought it over a moment and then said, "I'll come too. If you can get him in without being seen, I might as well be on his back. Besides, I don't relish the thought of spending the night out here. On top of that, if you drive your buckboard out of town, and come in empty, somebody might decide to look under your blanket, and there I'll be—and with only me in it, it sure as hell will look empty."

"Have it your way," he said.

"Here," I said, handing him some money. "This is in advance. I'll see that you get more later."

"Whatever you say, friend. Let's go."

We headed out and entered the town from the back. He had already opened the back doors to the livery stable, and we rode right in without being challenged. Mackenzie must have had some men *in* town looking out for me, but apparently hadn't set any men up on the rooftops to keep an eye out beyond the townline. I wondered if he just assumed that I had already found my way back into town, somehow.

It was a sure bet that he had somebody watching my

hotel, in case I tried to get in there to get my things, but that wasn't part of my plan. There was nothing in that room I couldn't do without for a while.

"I'll get the saddle off and rub him down," Freddie said when we dismounted. "I got a room back there with a cot you can use. You hungry?"

"No, I ate," I answered.

"Then you might as well pack it in for the night. In the morning you can tell me what your plans are, and we'll see what we can do about clearing you."

"I appreciate this, Freddie."

"Mackenzie ain't no friend of mine," he said, "and neither is Jed. You go on and get some sleep, I'll take good care of this brute for you."

Chapter Thirty-Three

In the morning Freddie offered to bring me some breakfast.

"I usually get breakfast and bring it back here to eat," he assured me. "I'll order a little extra. Nobody'll get suspicious."

I agreed and he came back with a plate heaped with scrambled eggs, bacon, and potatoes, and a pot of coffee. He found another plate in his room. there and divvied up the food.

"Has Jordan got some kind of a warehouse in town?" I asked as we were eating. "Where does he store his goods?"

"Right underneath his place, but how would he get a shipment of guns into town?"

"By marking the cartons flour, or salt, or anything else he deals in. I'd like to get a look at his storeroom."

"You don't think he'd have a batch of rifles down there now, do you?"

"Not if he's smart. He just killed his partner—"

"What?" he said, interrupting me. "I thought Indians killed Holt."

"That's what everyone is supposed to think. Jordan killed Holt, and if he's smart he'll stay away from guns for a while, especially since Holt has to be considered as

139

possibly having been the man selling the guns."

"Mackenzie's pretty set on you, the way I hear it."

"Mackenzie wants it to be me," I said, "but he's not going to get his way."

"That'll be a switch."

"Has he got Teal in town, or out?" I asked.

"Teal and his boys have been in town since yesterday, I guess looking for you."

"That means I can't move around at all during the day. I'm going to have to wait until tonight to try and get into that storeroom," I said as Freddie gathered up the remains of our breakfast. "Is there an entrance outside the place?"

He shrugged and said, "I don't know. I'll walk by there and find out."

"Also, maybe you can find out for me if he has a relief bartender."

"Holt used to do it, so if he's got one, he's gonna be somebody new."

"Well, see if you can find out. Where's Jordan live?"

"Upstairs from his place."

"Not in his old man's hotel, huh?"

"Shit, those two don't have nothing to do with each other," Freddie said. "You want me to go to your room and get your things?"

"You do that and somebody is sure to see you. They won't even have to follow you back here to figure out where I am. No, I can leave my things there. Nobody's going to touch them as long as they think there's a chance I might show up there myself."

"I'm gonna bring this stuff back to the café. If anybody comes in, stay out of sight. If it's a stranger, he'll wait, and if it's somebody from town, they'll help themselves."

I didn't need to be told to stay out of sight, but I agreed.

After he'd gone, I decided I needed a little more protection than my sidearm, so I went out to where my gear was to get my rifle. While I was out of Freddie's room, I heard voices near the front of the stable and I ducked into Duke's stall, which was all the way in the back. Peering between the slats of the stall, I could see Dutch Black and Jack Clinch enter.

"We checked this place out yesterday, Jack," Dutch was saying.

"We checked the whole damned town yesterday, Dutch, but we're still here today, ain't we? Joe wants this guy Adams found. The colonel is all over him about this. He wants that guy bad for making a fool of him."

"He sure did that," Dutch agreed. "The colonel looked mighty foolish—"

"You let him or Joe hear you say that, Dutch, and you'll be cleaning pots for months."

"I ain't afraid of them," Dutch replied.

"Yeah, sure. Listen, you want a drink?"

"Ain't we gonna check the stable?"

"We did, didn't we?" Clinch said, glancing around the inside of the stable. "I don't see nothing, do you?"

"No, but we ain't gone inside—"

Looking exasperated Clinch said, "You want that drink or not? Come on, I'm buying."

"Well, yeah, if you're buying . . ." Dutch started to answer, and his voice faded as they walked away.

Thanks to Jack Clinch's devotion to duty, he and Dutch Black were still alive. There was only one way I could have kept them from taking me—and then I would have had the problem of what to do with the bodies.

Chapter Thirty-Four

Sundown came as a great relief to me.

Freddie had discovered a back entrance to Jed Jordan's dugout cellar, behind the saloon and general store. It was locked, but he thought that we could get it open by taking the hinges off one of the wooden doors.

He had locked the front doors of the stable, and now we went out the back.

We ran along behind the buildings, climbing fences whenever necessary. He had discovered that while Dutch and Clinch patrolled one side of the street at night, Teal and Brady did the same on the other. Why they had not posted anyone in the back of the buildings I didn't know, but I was most grateful.

When we reached the rear of Jed Jordan's establishment, Freddie used a knife to pry up the hinges on one of the doors. The doors were not upright, but at an angle, and when he finally got the one open, we descended the steps and closed the door behind us. No one would notice the loose hinges unless they looked closely, and if the padlock was intact, why should they? The only problem we would have was if Jordan ran out of something and had to come downstairs to get it.

"There's probably a storm lamp at the bottom of these steps," I said. "You check the left and I'll check the right." Sure enough, I found it, hanging on a nail in the wall.

"Here it is," I said. I took out a match, lit it and touched it to the lamp. "You stay by the lamp," I instructed him. "If anyone opens the upstairs door, blow it out quick."

"Gotcha."

By the lamplight I could survey the room, now full of shadows thrown by the many cartons. If there were rifles in any of those cartons, as I hoped, all I'd have to do would be to get someone from the military to take a look down there—which in itself would be some feat.

First I checked the cartons that were already opened, but all I found were supplies for either the general store or the saloon.

The others were all nailed shut, so I was going to have to find something to pry them open with. I began looking around on the floor and found a hammer that Jordan himself probably used for the same purpose. As I bent over to pick it up, I kicked something with my left foot, and turned my head to see what it was.

"What did you find?" Freddie asked.

I stood up with the object in my hand and replied, "A box of cartridges."

It was a full, unopened box of cartridges, still wrapped in the manufacturer's wrapping paper.

"Would they fit the Winchester Seventy-threes?"

"They sure would," I replied, but the problem was that they would also fit a number of other weapons as well. All the box of cartridges did was convince me that I was on the right track, but it wouldn't convince the army, or a court of law.

I set the box back down on the floor, where Jordan had probably missed seeing it himself several times, and addressed myself to one of the unopened cartons. I tried slipping the clawed end of the hammer underneath the wooden top, but had no success. I would have to bang it a few times to get it under. If he heard it upstairs, we were in trouble, and if he didn't hear it the first time, he would probably hear it when I did it on one of the other cartons. But I had to give it a try.

I hit the hammer twice, forcing it under the carton top, and in that confined space it sounded as loud to me as two gunshots, but apparently no one upstairs heard it.

"Jesus," Freddie breathed.

The groan of the nails as I pried the top up was nothing compared to the initial noise, so I just ignored it until I got the top off. What was inside was something quite different from what I had expected. I picked one up and showed it to Freddie, whose eyes widened.

"What the hell is that, now?" he asked.

"That is a forty-five caliber Colt Peacemaker," I told him. "Colt's brand new handgun. It seems like our friend Mr. Jordan is not only selling Winchester Seventy-three rifles, but these as well."

"We got him, then," Freddie said.

"Well," I replied, putting the gun back, "these guns are here, but what's he intend to do with them?"

"Sell them to the Comanches, of course."

"The only Comanche I've ever seen carry a handgun is Quanah," I said. "Now, maybe Quanah is going to outfit his braves with these, but Jordan could just as well claim that he was going to sell them in his store."

"Then we don't have him," Freddie said, dejectedly.

"We might," I said. "You got a pencil?"

"Yeah, I think—yeah, here's one."

He gave me a nub of a pencil less than an inch long, but it would do. I found a piece of paper lying on a carton and took it.

"What are you gonna do?"

"I'm going to copy some of these serial numbers," I said. "Bring that lamp over here."

He took the lamp off of the wall and brought it over.

By its light I copied about a half a dozen of the serial numbers from those guns.

"That's it," I said, but at that point we heard a sound at the top of the steps.

"Douse the light!" I hissed.

Freddie blew the lamp out and he and I crouched down behind some cartons. We heard footsteps on the stairway, and then someone struck a match and lit a lamp. From my hiding place I watched Jed Jordan walk to an open carton and take out a couple of sacks of flour. I hoped he didn't notice that the top was loose on one of the gun cartons. I'd only had time to cover it without securing it again.

His eyes did scan the room briefly, as if trying to decide if there was anything else he needed while he was down there, but he did not seem to notice anything amiss—like the lamp missing from the other nail on the wall, which was still in Freddie's hand.

Finally, he seemed to decide that he had everything that he needed. He walked back to the foot of the stairs and blew out the lamp. I heard him hang it back on the wall, then he walked upstairs and closed the door.

"Jesus," Freddie said.

"Let me light that lamp again," I said.

He held the lamp up while I lit another match and touched it to the wick. When the room was once again lit I went about securing the top of the gun carton as best I could without making too much noise. I got the nails in the same holes and pushed the top down, and it seemed to help.

"Let's get out of here," I said.

"What do we do now?" Freddie asked as I blew out the lamp and hung it up again.

"Now it's time for you to send a telegram," I answered.

Chapter Thirty-Five

The next day I wrote out the telegram I wanted Freddie to send to my friend in Washington.

"Do these numbers mean anything to you?" he read aloud, and then rattled off the six numbers. He looked at me funny. "Is he gonna know what this means?"

"He will. He's assigned to the armory in Washington, so the only numbers I'd ask him about would be serial numbers."

"Well, how's he supposed to know it's from you?"

I pointed to the piece of paper in his hand and he looked at it again.

"You signed it 'G,'" he said.

"He'll know what it means," I assured him. It stood for Gunsmith, a name I hated, but one that might come in handy before this was all over.

"Now, wait until the regular man goes to lunch," I instructed him, "And then when the relief man sends it, wait for an answer."

"How do you know an answer will come back that quick?"

"If those guns are stolen, those numbers will catch my friend's eye right away. Then all I'll have to do is lay low until he gets here from Washington, with all the authority he needs to get me off the hook."

"I hope you know what you're doing," he said.

"I hope so, too, Freddie. Remember, try not to let anyone see you go in."

"You mean Teal and his friends?"

"Right. If you get caught, don't be brave and get yourself killed. Give up the telegram."

"And tell them you're over here?"

"You won't have to tell them. If they figure that you've been helping me, they'll know where to look."

"I'll do my best, Clint," he promised.

"I know you will, partner. Be careful."

"Right."

I didn't expect him back until later that afternoon, because he couldn't send the thing until after the regular telegraph operator went to lunch.

I thought about Quanah. I didn't think he'd want to try and teach his braves how to use a handgun at this stage of his war. Rifles were a different story, they worked on the same general principal as the bow and arrow. A handgun would be a whole new thing for an Indian. Still, those guns had to be stolen, whatever Jordan planned to do with them. He could have had other buys besides the Comanches. Actually, I didn't care what he intended to do with them, I just wanted them to be there when my friend, Captain Bill Fredericks, came to town in answer to my telegram. My friend was only a captain, and Mackenzie was a colonel, and a highly regarded one at that, but I hoped that my friend would come to town with enough authority behind him, like orders from Grant himself. Grant thought a lot of Mackenzie, but I hoped that wouldn't get in the way of his judgment on this particular matter.

I had no doubt that at some time or other Mackenzie must have been a good officer, but his obsessions were destroying him. His first was with Quanah, and his most recent one was me. He might do better for himself in another post, but he certainly wouldn't accept a transfer willingly. His pride wouldn't allow it.

A transfer would certainly do his wife a lot of good. It would get her back her husband, for one thing, and a woman like her shouldn't ever be dumped in a place like this, in the middle of nowhere. She belonged in a big town, where she could do all the things a good officer's wife was supposed to do, like have tea and attend socials. I hoped that she wouldn't get it in her mind to leave with me when—and if—I finally pulled out. I'd hate to have a man like Mackenzie on my trail for the rest of my life.

I must have dozed off, and it was the sound of Duke's whinny that brought me back to my senses. Someone was in the barn, and my hand hovered near my gun until I heard Freddie's voice saying, "It's me."

He came into the room, carrying what looked like a telegram.

"Is that the answer?" I asked.

"Yeah, but it's only one word. I sure hope your friend understood."

"What's it say?"

He looked at it and read, " 'Jackpot'."

I smiled and assured him, "He understood, and he's on his way."

"What you gonna do in the meantime?"

"Try to stay alive."

Chapter Thirty-Six

I'd been in hiding for three days, when something happened that made me regret involving Freddie in my troubles. He came in with dinner and wearing a troubled look on his face.

"What's the matter?" I asked.

"We may have trouble," he said, putting the food down on the small wooden table he kept in his room.

"What do you mean?"

"Andy Tyler."

I snorted and said, "That useless sheriff? What kind of a threat could he possibly be?"

"He's got a big mouth, that's what kind of threat," he said. "He was in the café last night, and again tonight, and tonight he remarked that I been ordering enough food for two."

I frowned and asked, "What did you tell him?"

"I told him that watching him work so hard gave me a big appetite," he answered. "He didn't think that was so funny, I'm afraid."

"Okay, let's not get all worried over this. Go back to ordering your usual meals. And if Tyler shows up we can take care of him."

"You mean kill him?"

"No, just put him out of action for a while. What are

151

people going to think if they don't see Tyler around for a while?"

"That's he's curled up somewhere with a bottle, I guess."

"Good. Then we won't ruin his reputation any."

"It ain't him I'm worried about," he said. I knew what he meant before he even said it.

"What if he mentions it to Teal and his boys?"

"So we'll have to be alert," I said, trying to play it down some, "but let's not panic."

"Sure, easy for you to say."

"Relax, Freddie. Sit down and eat your dinner."

"Probably won't have no appetite," he mumbled, sitting down, but he went ahead and ate his fair share, so I knew his appetite wasn't bothered none.

I was more worried than I let on to him, however. If the sheriff talked, and Teal came to the stable with Clinch, Brady *and* Dutch Black, there wouldn't be any way out for me except to kill them before they killed me. After that, I'd have a murder charge hanging over my head.

Actually, Freddie ate more than his fair share, because I was the one who didn't have much of an appetite.

"Freddie, listen," I said as he gathered up the plates and utensils to return to the café.

"What?"

"Why don't you find someplace else to spend the night tonight?" I suggested. He had been sleeping in one of the stalls on some hay since he'd given—or rented—his room to me.

"You all of a sudden worried?" he asked.

"It should only be another couple of days," I said. "All I'm suggesting is that you stay out of the way for that length of time, just in case something should happen."

"I got a gun around here somewhere, you know," he said, looking around to see if he could locate it. "I ain't afraid of them soldier boys."

"I'm not saying you're afraid, Freddie, but I'd hate to see you get killed trying to help me. You've done enough already."

"As long as you know I ain't afraid to back ya," he said.

"Believe me, I know you're not afraid," I said. "You can find someplace else to spend the next couple of nights, can't you?"

"Yeah, maybe with one of them ladies over at the whorehouse," he said, looking eager.

"This town's got a cathouse?" I asked, surprised.

"A couple of girls is all," he said. "I been there once or twice."

"Well then, you go over there again," I said, handing him some money. "On me."

He took the money and rubbed his mouth, saying, "Well, I don't mind telling you I wouldn't mind . . ."

"Go ahead, Freddie," I urged him. "Have a good time."

"I'll be seeing you in the morning, then," he said.

"Sure, I'll be here," I assured him.

He left with his mind full of visions of Fort Sill's two-girl whorehouse.

As I found out later, that might have been the last thought of his life.

Chapter Thirty-Seven

Thinking about Freddie spending the night in a whorehouse did not make it any easier for me to be cooped up in that stable for another night. I was very tempted to slip out the back and see if Sheila Mackenzie was home alone again.

About an hour after dark, I decided that I had to get out, at least to walk around outside for a little while. I decided that instead of walking aimlessly, I'd go looking for Dancing Willow, who by now must have been very worried about her sister. I was sure I'd be able to move among the Indians without being spotted by the soldiers.

I slipped carefully out the back door, not locking the front because that would have looked suspicious that early in the evening.

On foot I worked my way around the town and entirely around the fort, keeping very close to the base of the walls so as not to be seen from above.

Peering upward, I could make out one of the sentries standing on top of the wall. As he turned his head to light a cigarette, I left the cover of the wall and moved in among the collection of teepees. By the time he looked out again, I was hidden behind one of them. As he patrolled his wall, I moved in among the teepees looking for the one that housed Dancing Willow and the people who were caring for her in Dancing Fawn's absence.

I called out in turn at each teepee, only loud enough to be heard by the people inside, and all I called out was Dancing Willow's name.

At the fifth teepee I tried, I got an answer from within. It was barely audible, but I heard it because I was looking for it.

"Willow," I called again.

The flap of the teepee came back and she stuck her head out, looking puzzled. When she saw me, the look of puzzlement changed to one of delight.

"Clint," she said, having learned to say my name.

Now that I was there with her, I wasn't all that sure I'd be able to communicate with her. I was going to pull her out of the teepee, but I decided instead to go inside.

Inside there was one other person, an older woman who could have been anywhere from thirty to fifty. She looked frightened at my appearance, but Willow said something to her in their own language that seemed to put her at ease.

When I spoke, I spoke to the older woman, not to Dancing Willow.

"Do you speak English?" I asked her.

She hesitated so long I thought that she couldn't understand me, but then she nodded her head jerkily and I heaved a sigh of relief.

As simply as possible, I explained to her that she should tell Willow that her sister was safe with Quanah, and that very soon I would be taking her to Quanah as well, so that she could be with her sister.

As the woman relayed this information to Dancing Willow her eyes began to glow with excitement and pleasure, and she looked at me and nodded vigorously.

I explained to the woman that Willow would have to

always be alert, because when I came for her it could be in the quiet of the night, or it could be during the day and in a hurry. Willow nodded her head that she understood this and she put her hands against my chest in a gesture of thanks. I patted her hands, and told them that I had to leave.

I slipped out of the teepee and retraced all of my steps until I slipped back into the livery stable through the back doors.

As soon as I got inside I sensed that something wasn't right. I slipped my gun from my holster and advanced into the stable slowly and carefully.

First I checked Duke, and he was okay, but he rolled his eyes, indicating that he had been spooked, and not long ago, either.

Someone had been in the stable while I was gone, that was for sure. Had it simply been an evening customer? Or had it been either the sheriff, or Teal and his men?

Perhaps I had finally lucked out. Maybe they had picked the exact time I was out of the stable to check it thoroughly. It could have been that, looking for me, they had not even taken a close look at Duke, and had not recognized him as my horse. I might have been home free for the next couple of days, safe in the stable because I'd been out when they checked it.

I checked every stall, and then I went above and checked there, too, but there was no one else in there with me. I holstered by gun and descended back to the main floor, satisfied that I was alone.

It wasn't until I went back into Freddie's room that I realized that I wasn't alone at all.

On the cot, with his head twisted at an odd angle, lay Freddie, a man whose last name I didn't even know.

He was dead.

Chapter Thirty-Eight

I crouched down next to the cot and silently apologized to him for getting him killed. There was no doubt in my mind that he was dead because he chose to help me. The manner in which he was killed told me that Dutch Black had done it, which put Joe Teal behind it.

Speak of the devil and up he pops.

"Adams," Teal's voice called from out of the darkness. He was calling from in front of the stable. "We know you're in there, Adams!"

I didn't answer, just stayed where I was and pulled my gun.

"Don't think about slipping out the back way, Adams. We've got every exit covered!" Teal informed me. I had no doubt that he was right. With four of them, they'd be able to cover the entire stable.

"I'm sending Dutch Black in unarmed, Adams. You can shoot him down if you want, but you'll hang for killing an unarmed man."

I remembered what Freddie had told me about facing Dutch Black. Shoot him right away, don't let him get a chance to put his hands on me, but Teal had that figured. I couldn't very well gun down an unarmed man, to say nothing of an unarmed United States soldier. I might as well turn myself in now if I was planning on doing that.

"I told you we'd test you with Dutch, Adams," Teal reminded me, "so here he comes. Good luck—you're sure as hell going to need it."

I holstered my gun and looked around for something to use on Dutch. Maybe he'd change his mind, I thought, and not take Teal's word for it that I wouldn't shoot him on sight. That thought faded from my mind as Dutch's gigantic form filled the doorway.

He looked larger than he'd ever looked to me before. Legs like tree trunks, heavily-muscled shoulders and arms.

"I'll twist off your head, like I done your friend," he said, walking into the barn.

I left the small room and went out to meet him, a seething rage building up inside of me. A rage at Teal, for knowing I wouldn't shoot, a rage at Dutch for having killed Freddie, and a rage at myself for ever having stopped in Fort Sill.

"Come on, little man," he said, "make it easy on yourself. You don't want a lot of pain, do you?"

I stopped walking and he kept coming. When he was close enough I launched a vicious kick, catching him on the shin with the toe of my boot. He grunted and staggered back, but he had not howled the way a normal man would have. I had hoped to catch him with his weight on one leg, so I could kick that one out from under him, but that wasn't to be. He kept both feet planted firmly on the ground, and didn't even rub what I knew had to be an aching shin.

"That's the best you can do, huh?" he asked, coming back at me slowly.

I waited until he was close enough and then launched another kick at the same exact spot. If nothing else, after he killed me he was going to have a wicked bruise on that shin.

"Damn," he breathed, backtracking again. "You

keep that up, Adams, you're gonna make me mad."

"You won't get mad, Dutch," I said to him. "Joe Teal is not in here to tell you to, and you don't do anything unless Teal tells you to, and shows you how. You're a moron, Dutch."

"No, I ain't."

"Yes, you are. You ain't got the brains of a grizzly bear," I taunted him.

"Don't make me mad, Adams. I'm gonna kill you anyway, but if you made me mad I'm gonna make you suffer."

"You're nothing, Dutch," I said, circling him. I knew I had one thing on him, and that was speed. If I could use that, I could wear him down.

I moved in and threw a quick right at his belly, but that was an obvious waste of time. My knuckles bounced off his stomach, which was as hard as a .washboard.

"You keep circling around like that, mister, you're gonna make yourself dizzy. I'll just wait until you fall down and then squash you."

"Don't bang your foot down too hard, Dutch," I told him, "you might hurt your brain—if you've got one."

"I got a brain," he insisted.

"Yeah, in your big toe. Maybe I'll just stomp on it for you," I offered.

"Come and try," he said, grinning tightly. There was a mad glint in his eye. He'd killed once tonight, and he was looking forward to doing it again.

I moved in and feinted with my left, and when he moved to block it I hit him in the face with my right, accomplishing no more than bruising my knuckles. He didn't even blink.

"Nothing," he said. "You got nothing, Adams. I'm coming for you now."

He started to move in on me and I tried the kick

again, but he was smarter than I figured. He caught my foot and twisted it, throwing me to the ground. Instead of holding onto it, though, he let it go and tried to stomp me into the ground. I rolled away and avoided his massive foot, which probably would have broken me in half had it landed on me.

I scrambled to my feet and found my back against one of the stalls. He advanced on me with his arms held away from his body, so I could get by. As he closed on me, I grabbed a saddle that was sitting on the stall and threw it at him. He swatted it away with one hand, and that's the way I went to get away from him, ducking underneath his huge arm. I got behind him and peppered his kidneys with rights and lefts before he could turn, but as he did turn he swung his right arm backhanded and caught me flush on the right cheek, knocking me for a loop. As I hit the ground everything threatened to go dark on me, but that would have meant sure death. I wouldn't even have been awake while he twisted my neck the way he did Freddie's.

I fought off the darkness and the buzzing in my ears, shaking my head to try and clear it and rolling away from him, trying to stay out of his reach until I could see again.

As I started rolling he threw a kick and it was only the fact that I was moving that kept it from caving in my ribs when it landed. As it was, it lifted me clean off the ground and I landed with a jar that seemed to be the chief reason my head cleared up. Holding my elbow against my side, at least now I could see him as he moved towards me, readying another kick.

I ducked under his boot so that his legs actually slid along my back, and when I stood up straight, it threw him off balance, and he fell to the ground. I moved in as fast as I could and tried to return the favor with a kick. I landed at least one kick solidly and was satisfied to hear him grunt. As he pushed against the ground with his hands to get to his feet, I sent another kick at him, hoping to catch him in the head, but he moved his head to the side and I caught one of his shoulders. He scrambled to his feet and I backed away.

He didn't seem anymore than just dirty, while my left side felt as if it was on fire, as did my lungs. He wasn't even breathing hard.

"At least you're making it interesting," he admitted, "but now I'm gonna kill you."

As he moved in on me, I lowered my head and tried to surprise him by running at him instead of away from him. The top of my head hit his stomach with little effect, and then I felt his powerful arms wrap around my body.

He had me around the waist and lifted me off the ground. My left arm was pinned to my side, though my right arm was still free. I tried to break his hold unsuccessfully, and then I started hitting him in the face with my fist, but that also seemed to have no effect. His face was clenched with the effort of squeezing the life out of me, and I felt that I had no choice now but to use my gun or die.

I reached for my gun and, before shooting him, decided to try one more thing. I raised my hand high with the gun in my hand and brought it crashing down on his head. His arms went weak and I dropped to the floor as his hands flew to his head, to protect it. I got quickly to my feet, drew my hand back, and laid my shooting iron alongside the left side of his face, ripping his cheek open from just next to his eye to the point of his chin. He screamed and the blood poured down the front of his shirt, but amazingly he stayed on his feet.

He shook his head, splattering his blood around, and some of it landed on me. I switched the gun from my right to my left, stepped in while he attempted to clear the blood from his eyes, and laid it flat against the right side of his face. It didn't cut him this time, but it landed solidly and I felt the jolt up my entire arm. He swayed, his eyes wide and glassy, and then his eyes rolled up into his head and he went crashing over backwards and lay still.

I bent over him with my gun ready, but he was out cold, and I was still alive and glad of it.

I sat down in the middle of the floor and worked at getting my breath back. After a few moments, Teal's voice came from outside again.

"Dutch, did you get him?" he called out.

I didn't answer the first time because I still didn't have my breath back, but when he called out the same thing a second time, I didn't answer because I decided to let him think what he wanted.

"Dutch!" he shouted stridently, but still I didn't answer, and Dutch wouldn't be answering for a long time. His breathing was regular now. He was healthy enough, he was just totally unconscious and would be for some time.

I went back into Freddie's room, where I covered his body with a blanket. Then I grabbed a rag and went back out to where Dutch lay. Not that he deserved it, but I pushed the dirty rag against his bleeding face, then turned his head so that the rag was pinned between his head and the ground. Eventually, that would staunch the bleeding, keeping him from bleeding to death.

"Adams," Teal called again, obviously giving up on his man. "I don't know how you did it, Adams, but you got Dutch. We're still out here, though, and we can wait longer than you can. Daylight comes and we'll come in and get you. The colonel wants you alive, Adams," he informed me, "but I don't. I'll just tell him you resisted, started shooting at us, and we were forced to gun you down. You ain't got much time left to live, Adams, so say your prayers."

I stayed quiet, not bothering to answer him. I didn't want to waste my energy talking, because I was going to need it to get out of there, and if I was going to make it out, I would have to do it before daylight.

Chapter Thirty-Nine

If I got out of there, I was going to have to get out
with Duke and one other horse. I couldn't forget my
promise to take Willow to her sister, or my debt to
Dancing Fawn.

There weren't enough horses in there for me to stam-
pede them out and make it out among them. I looked
around, found some cans of turpentine and, in the back,
I found an old buckboard. It hadn't been used in some
time, but it was in one piece. The germ of an idea started
to grow, and I went and got one of the horses to hitch to
the buckboard.

That done, I grabbed a pitchfork and started pitching
hay onto it. Once I had it piled up high, I grabbed the
cans of turpentine and doused the wood of the buckboard. I wouldn't have to douse the hay, that would
burn naturally. I was sorry about the horse, but there
was no other way to do this. I just had to hope somebody would get to the poor animal before he got burned.

I saddled Duke up, and then picked out what looked
to be the best horse of the others for Dancing Willow.
Then I led the lone horse hitched to the buckboard out
into the center of the floor. The last part was the
hardest, and that was getting Dutch Black up onto a
horse. There's a lot of strength in desperation though,

and I finally got him astride one of the poor animals, who rolled his eyes at having to bear all that weight. I found some baling wire and used it to make sure Dutch sat up as straight as he could. I walked Duke and the other horse to the back doors, and then I was ready.

I took out a match and, lighting it, threw it onto the buckboard. The hay caught, and as it burned the turpentine in the wood caught. When the buckboard was in flames I let the frightened horse go and he ran out through the front doors without any prompting. Right behind him I sent the horse bearing Dutch Black, and then I went and mounted Duke and took off out the back doors.

I heard some shouting from the front, and then some gunshots as they shot at the poor unconscious Dutch, who they probably thought was me.

Apparently, the one who had been stationed in the back had chosen to try and run through the barn to see what was happening out front, and as I rode out with Duke and the other horse, we virtually knocked the man down—either Clinch or Brady, I couldn't say for sure—and rode over him. There was some more shooting, but none of it seemed to be coming my way.

Leading the second horse, I circled Duke around the town, heading for the reservation. The flaming buckboard and all of the shooting would attract a lot of attention, and some of it, I hoped, would come from the fort so that no one would see me riding among those teepees, looking for Dancing Willow.

She had apparently obeyed me when I told her to be alert, because she was standing outside as I rode up. She nimbly scrambled astride the horse I'd brought for her, and we took off into the night, away from all the commotion behind the fort.

Chapter Forty

I had to keep Duke back some, to make sure that Dancing Willow was in front of us and not behind us. Still, we were traveling at a good pace, and Willow seemed to know exactly where she was going.

We rode that way until dawn, and then I decided to give the horses a rest. I had some beef jerky in my saddlebag, which was who knows how old, but I gave some to Willow and I chewed on some. The horse I'd chosen for her was a decent one, but his sides were heaving and he was blowing some. I was going to have to give him a decent rest so we wouldn't run him into the ground. Duke, on the other hand, was breathing just fine, and might have even been impatient to get moving again.

Willow and I couldn't talk at all, so she just spent all her time smiling at me, and I smiled back and nodded, to indicate that everything would be all right. She was seemingly unconcerned and not in need of my assurances. Maybe I was assuring myself more than I was her.

I kept a sharp eye out behind us, because over that flat land I'd be able to see if anyone was coming up behind us while they were still miles away. I had no doubt that after Teal reported to Mackenzie, he'd send someone out after us, and might even come himself. By now he must have been tired of me thumbing my nose at him and his men.

After we rested we hadn't gone two miles more when her horse stepped in a hole, throwing her as it fell to the ground. His right foreleg broke with an audible snap, so I had to put him out of his misery. Willow was unhurt, so I hoisted her onto my saddle behind me and we rode double. Her weight was negligible, but over a long haul it would probably reduce the ground we'd cover. As long as I kept Duke at a moderate pace, we'd be all right. If Mackenzie was behind us, however, and traveling fast, he might catch up to us before we hit the Plains.

As we rode along, I wondered what the hell I was going to do after I left Willow with her people. Getting back to town and the fort alive wouldn't be easy, not after last night. For all I knew, Dutch had been killed when they shot at him thinking he was me, and Jack Clinch could have been killed when we rode over him. I could have two counts of murder waiting for me at Fort Sill.

One alternative was to drop her off and then keep riding until I got into Mexico, but I didn't relish spending the rest of my life in Mexico, knowing that the minute I crossed the border I was subject to arrest. And who knew how many bounty hunters would cross the border for a chance at the Gunsmith, ex-lawman turned fugitive.

I didn't like the sound of that. I had to get back somehow and clear myself. And I had to be there when Fredericks showed up. There was no one there now to tell him where the stolen guns were. Without the evidence of those guns in Jed Jordan's basement, I didn't have a prayer of being cleared.

I would have to go back, but first things first. I had to deliver Fawn into the hands of Quanah and her sister.

And that would have to happen soon, I realized. Because I took a look over my shoulder as we rode on towards the Staked Plains and was sure I saw a dust cloud behind us. It would have to be a fairly large force of men to raise that kind of dust in this barren country, and that size company would have to be led by Mackenzie himself.

Mackenzie must have figured that he'd either catch me, or I'd lead him to Quanah, and he'd want to be on hand for either event.

Mile after mile we covered, and they kept getting closer and closer. I could have run Duke full out and put some distance between us, but if they kept coming steadily, they'd have to make up the ground while we rested. It would be pushing Duke for no reason. Mackenzie was obsessed, and he wouldn't stop for a few exhausted animals.

When we finally got to the Plains, I wondered if Mackenzie would follow us in. Apparently, he had—I figured that if we were alone Quanah's braves would have approached by now and taken Willow. But if we had a company on our tail, they would probably be playing it safe. They wouldn't come down from the escarpments until they were sure they equaled or outnumbered the soldiers.

I decided that the best thing to do was find someplace where I could make some kind of a stand, and wait for Quanah's men to arrive. Eventually, we came to such a spot. It was a steep arroyo where I could leave Duke and Willow at the bottom while I climbed back to the top with my rifle. I had no intention of picking off any of the soldiers; all I wanted to do was make them reluctant to come any further. Of course, if they rushed me, they'd have me, but I was hoping they would think at least twice before deciding to do that.

I rode into the arroyo and tried to communicate to

Willow what I wanted her to do. When I thought she understood, I took my rifle and climbed back up to the top to wait for Mackenzie to arrive.

Mackenzie, and Quanah.

Chapter Forty-One

As it turned out, they were only half an hour behind us, and as they approached the arroyo, I fired on them, kicking up some dust directly in front of Mackenzie's horse. The animal reared, but Mackenzie controlled it and signaled his men to dismount. They took up cover wherever they could, some of them just laying flat in the open. There were about twenty-five of them; I recognized only Mackenzie, Teal and Brady.

I fired once again for good measure, to keep their heads down, and then I slid down out of sight. Let them wonder for a while where the shots had come from, and who fired them.

I lay on my back and looked up at the steep escarpments on both sides. I couldn't see anyone, but I knew there had to be at least some Comanches up there watching us. I hoped they would show themselves soon, and that there would be enough of them to make Mackenzie retreat.

I turned over to check on the soldier boys. They hadn't moved since they dismounted. They probably thought that the shots had come from up above, and as long as they thought that, nobody was going to look my way. Of course, if I had to fire again it would give away my position, and they would probably realize that it was me—and not Quanah—shooting at them. I'd hold off firing again for as long as I possibly could.

I heard a noise behind me and turned quickly, rifle ready, but it was only Willow.

"Don't sneak up on me like that," I said.

She didn't understand, but she started pointing above us, trying to tell me something.

"What did you see?" I asked.

She couldn't answer, just kept pointing, and I had to assume that, being an Indian, she knew that there were Indians above us. Maybe she saw them, or maybe she just felt them, but she knew they were there.

"Well, if they're here," I said, "I wish they'd show themselves. I just hope Mackenzie isn't too obsessed to turn back when he realizes he's outnumbered."

I turned to check them again, and there was some movement. He seemed to be delegating a few of his men to move up, probably to draw fire so he could see where it was coming from. Willow crawled up next to me to take a look, and I let her stay. It was her life, too.

I watched as a few of the soldiers began to crawl forward on their bellies. I could see Mackenzie with his face turned upwards, watching for any sign of movement from there. From my angle, it would be very hard to fire in front of them. On this hard ground, a bullet could very well skip along and hit one of them in the face, which is something I didn't want to do. I had no quarrel with twenty-two of those twenty-five men, and I didn't even want to hurt the three with whom I did have a quarrel.

I leveled my rifle but did not fire as the three men continued to move forward with their rifles in their hands. If they kept coming, I would have to fire over their heads.

As I was taking aim, Willow tapped my arm and I looked at her. She was pointing behind us, and as I turned my head to look, I felt a chill.

There was Quanah, sitting high and tall astride his horse. I turned to look at Mackenzie, who had also seen Quanah. Many of his men were looking up now, too, and as I looked up I saw that both sides of the escarpment were full of Comanches.

Mackenzie and his men were hopelessly outnumbered, and surrounded on three sides. Willow and I were right in the middle, in more ways than one.

The tension in the air was incredible, as both sides just sat there and stared at each other.

This is going to turn into a massacre, I thought. There was only one way to avoid it, and that was for me to stand up and go with Mackenzie. I had to hope that he was enough soldier to want to take me back to Fort Sill to face charges, and with luck, Captain Fredericks would have arrived from Washington, waiting to help me clear everything up.

I stood up and walked out of the arroyo, facing Mackenzie and his men. I made a big show of dropping my rifle to the ground and putting my hands out away from my body. Joe Teal rose and aimed his rifle at me, but Mackenzie knocked it away.

"I'm not here to murder him," I heard him tell Teal, who shook his head and lowered his rifle.

"Adams, walk forward," Mackenzie said. Then he ordered his men to keep an eye on the Indians. I approached him and stopped a few feet in front of him.

"Drop your gun," Mackenzie said.

"Not a chance, Mackenzie," I said. "That's not why I walked out here."

"Then why?"

"To save your life, and the lives of your men. You're here because of me, and I don't want a massacre on my conscience."

Mackenzie thought about that and then said, "What do you propose?"

"I propose that I get you and your men out of here in one piece."

"And what about you?"

"Will you leave without me?"

"After coming all this way? Never!"

The glint was still there in his eyes, and both objects of his obsession were right here in front of him. If his men were killed, he'd be as much to blame as I was.

"All right," I said. "I'll go back with you, colonel. You can fight Quanah another day, when you're not so hopelessly outnumbered."

He looked as if he were about to respond to that, but then his eyes flashed upward and straight ahead, and he assessed the situation as a soldier should.

"Do what you can," he said, and he wasn't happy about having to say those words.

"I'm going to send the girl out to them, then I'm going to get my horse and ride towards you. When you see me on my horse, mount up your men, and be ready to run for it if we have to."

"Right."

I turned and he called, "Adams."

"Yeah?"

"You're going back under arrest."

"I know it," I said, and that seemed to puzzle him. "Keep your men under control, colonel, especially Teal. One shot and we could all be finished."

I turned and walked back to pick up my fallen rifle, then I extended my hand to Willow and brought her up into view.

"Go to your people," I told her, and then tried to say the same thing with my hands. She got the message, gave me a hug around my waist, and then rode down into the arroyo and up the other side. Quanah rode forward and met her half-way, hoisted her up onto his pony with him, and went back to his position. I went down into the arroyo, walked Duke up to the top, then mounted up. I looked back and locked eyes with Quanah, but his told me nothing. I gigged Duke's side and started towards Mackenzie and his men. He spoke to them and they all began to mount up. He mounted his horse and stood there facing me, waiting for me.

As I drew up alongside of him I said, "Let's go . . . slowly. At the first sign of trouble we take off like the devil was on our tail."

"He will be," Mackenzie said. He turned his animal around and rode with me. His men turned their horses and when we took the lead, they followed.

"Don't look back," I said.

"I know how to act with Indians, Adams," he replied tightly.

"Good," I said. "Then you tell me what's next."

"If they start after us, we'll hear them," he said. "They'll start screaming like the savages they are."

"Will I make it back to the fort, Mackenzie," I asked him, "or will Teal put a bullet in me before we get there?"

"With a little luck, Adams, we'll all make it back to the fort," he answered. "When I get you there, you'll stand trial for treason and a few other charges."

"When we get back I'll clear myself, Mackenzie."

"That remains to be seen."

Suddenly, from behind us came the wild yells and screams of the Comanches who, I had to admit, did sound pretty savage at that moment. I figured they had their reasons.

"First we'll have to get back," Mackenzie said.

"Right," I agreed.

We kicked our horses into full gallop.

Chapter Forty-Two

We rode hell-bent for leather until we were off the Staked Plains, and then Quanah and his braves gave it up and we were able to slow down to a more reasonable pace.

"They didn't even fire a shot at us," Mackenzie remarked, looking puzzled.

"Maybe they just wanted us to get off the Plains," I suggested.

"Maybe." He held up his hand for his men to stop, and then turned to me. "Your guns, Adams."

"What?"

"I want your guns."

"Hey, man, I saved your life back there," I reminded him.

"And I'm grateful, but you're under arrest. There are two guns pointed at your back, and I want your weapons."

One of those guns had to be Teal's, and he didn't need much provocation to shoot me in the back, so I handed Mackenzie my rifle and my pistol.

"You're making a big mistake, Mackenzie. I know who's been selling the guns to the Indians, and I know where there's a shipment of stolen handguns right now."

"Handguns?"

I nodded. "New Colt Peacemakers."

"And I'll bet you could bring me right to them, couldn't you?" Mackenzie asked sarcastically.

"Now wait a minute—"

"They'd be worth your freedom to you, wouldn't they?"

"Mackenzie—"

"That's the last word I want to hear from you until we get back to Fort Sill, Adams. If you speak again, I'll have you bound and gagged."

I believed him, and kept quiet the rest of the ride back, hoping again that I'd have word from Fredericks.

When we got back there was no sign of Fredericks, and Mackenzie had me thrown in the stockade. That wouldn't have been so bad, except that my guards were Sergeant Joe Teal and Corporal Sam Brady. I just hoped that Mackenzie had given them orders not to kill me.

They had to have their cheap shots, though.

"You made fools of us last night, Adams," Teal said.

"Did I? How's Dutch, by the way. Has he got a headache?"

"You're lucky we didn't kill Dutch when he came out of that barn wired to that horse," Teal said. "And Jack Clinch got off with a broken arm, or else you'd be up on a murder charge."

"Guess I should consider myself fortunate," I agreed.

I was lying on the cot in my cell, and Teal was leaning on the bars outside.

"Where's your other buddy, Brady?"

"Sam? He went to get you your dinner. We treat prisoners right here, you know."

"That's comforting."

"And here he is, with your dinner," Teal said as I heard a door opening.

"You got Mr. Adams's dinner, Sam?" he asked.

"I sure do," Brady said from out of sight.

"Well, let me open up the door so's you can give it to him," Teal offered. Brady came into view carrying a tray, but Brady had barely taken two steps into the cell when he threw the tray and the contents in my face. Whatever it was was damn hot, and I covered my face with my hands.

One of them hit me in the stomach, and as I doubled up I took another punch in the head. After that, it was kind of crowded in the cell, with the two of them working me over with combinations of punches and kicks.

Later, I woke up on the floor of the cell, with the contents of the tray still splattered around me. I pulled myself up and leaned against the cot. I checked myself out and aside from a few bruises and a split lip, I seemed to be all in one piece.

While I was sitting there, I heard a door open and then footsteps. Mackenzie stared down at me through the bars.

"What happened to this man?" he asked.

Teal stood next to him.

"He's real clumsy," Teal answered. "Brady gave him his dinner and he tripped, dropped the tray and hit his head. He didn't seem to be hurt too bad, so we let him sleep it off."

Mackenzie didn't believe it, but he said to Teal, "That's all," and the sergeant went back to his post by the door.

"You ready to confess, Adams?" he asked.

I moved my jaw around to work out the kinks, and then said, "To what?"

"The guns."

"I told you, I have never sold guns to the Indians, but I can tell you who has."

"Oh, really? Who?"

"Jed Jordan."

"Who told you that—Quanah?" he asked.

"As a matter of fact, he did," I replied.

"Well, in that case, I guess I should open the door and let you walk out, right? I mean, the word of a savage . . ."

"You keep referring to them as savages, Mackenzie," I said. "Try looking around you and tell me what you see right here in the fort."

"I see my men, Adams," he snapped back, "whose lives are in danger because you've armed Quanah and his braves with Winchester Seventy-threes."

"I told you—"

"Yes, I know what you told me. Jed Jordan is guilty, and you're innocent. What else are you innocent of, Adams?" he asked. "Sleeping with another man's wife? Tell me Jed Jordan is the one who's been doing that, too."

I had no answer to that. I could only wonder how he'd found out.

"That's okay, Adams. I'm sure if you spend enough time in here, you'll come to your senses and tell the truth."

He turned to Teal and said, "Take good care of this man, sergeant. Someone should go in there and clean him off."

"Yes, sir," Teal answered.

"You let the sergeant know when you're ready to talk, Adams," Mackenzie told me.

"I've told you—" I began, but he walked away and out of the building.

Teal came over when his superior was gone and said, "Look at you. Wouldn't that food have done much more good inside of you than outside?"

"Why don't you come in here and say that?" I said.

He smiled and said, "You'd like that, wouldn't you? Don't worry," he assured me, "we'll talk again . . . real soon."

Chapter Forty-Three

As it turned out, Teal, Brady and I talked again . . . and again . . . and again. They were good at what they did. The initial split lip was the only mark they put on me where it would show. Everything else was administered below the shoulders and above the ankles.

After two days, if I had been selling guns to the Indians, I would have confessed. As it was, I was thinking about confessing to it anyway. Everytime I did think that way, though, I imagined what Mackenzie's face would look like when he realized that he'd won.

Once or twice they allowed me to eat my meals, but I still felt as if I hadn't eaten in days. I was unshaven and unwashed, and I was starting to wonder if I was ever going to get out.

Then I got a surprise for breakfast—finally, a *pleasant* surprise.

"Stand at attention, soldier!" I heard a familiar voice order.

"Yes, sir," Teal replied, and I heard his chair scrape back as he stood up. .

I was lying on my back on my cot and I lifted my head to see who the new visitor was.

"Clint," the voice called.

I wiped a hand across my eyes and tried to make out

the face through the bars.

"Open the door, soldier," the voice commanded.

"I'm sorry, sir," I heard Teal say. "I can't do that without orders from the colonel—"

"Read this," the voice said. I heard papers rustling and the new voice added, "I am acting for President Grant in this matter, and my authority comes directly from him. Now open this damned door!"

"Yes, sir," Teal said. I heard the key scrape in the lock and then the door swung open.

A familiar face stood above me, looking down, and Captain Bill Fredericks said, "Jesus, Clint, what the hell did they do to you?"

"Hi, Bill," I said, my voice barely a whisper.

He turned and said, "Sergeant, I want a doctor here in five minutes, or by God, you'll need one worse than he does!"

"Yes, sir!"

Bill squatted next to me and said, "Clint, are you all right? Can you walk?"

"I don't know," I said. "I haven't tried lately. Did you just get into town?"

"I got in last night" he replied, "but I just found out you were in here. Did Mackenzie order this?"

"I guess so."

"Then he's finished."

"Help me up," I said.

Instead of doing that, he placed both his hands against my chest and said, "Wait for the doctor."

I didn't feel like arguing the matter.

"It's good to see you," I said, sincerely.

"It's good to see you, too, but, my God, what did you do to deserve this?"

I licked my dry, cracked lips and then said, "I saved their lives."

Chapter Forty-Four

The doctor checked me over in the cell and pronounced that I had no broken bones. He suggested I stay off my feet for a few days.

"There should be a bottle of whiskey on the desk outside," I told Bill.

"I'll get it."

He brought it back and I took a couple of healthy pulls at it, letting the liquor burn its way through my body, waking me up.

"I feel better already," I said, starting to get up. Bill reached, but this time it was to help me up, not hold me down.

"Do you want to go to the hotel?" he asked.

"What about Mackenzie?"

"We can take care of him later. I'd like to talk about the guns."

"Let's take care of Mackenzie now," I said, "and then we can talk about the guns whileswe eat."

"Okay. Lean on me."

With his help I walked across the compound to Mackenzie's office, and when we gained an audience with him, we found Joe Teal already there.

"That's all, sergeant," Fredericks told him, and Teal left the room.

"What's the meaning of this?" Mackenzie demanded. "What right have you to supersede my authority and release this man, captain?"

Mackenzie made sure that he put a heavy connotation on "captain," but that didn't bother Bill Fredericks.

Bill reached into his jacket and produced his orders, handing them to Mackenzie, who snatched them away and read them.

"As you can see, colonel, my orders come directly from the President. If I should decide that you have abused your authority as commander of Fort Sill, I am to relieve you immediately, pending a hearing—"

"I can read, captain!" Mackenzie snapped viciously.

"I didn't mean to imply that you couldn't, sir," Fredericks responded politely.

"This is preposterous! In what way do you feel I have abused my authority?" Mackenzie demanded.

"I think torturing a prisoner would be good for starters, sir."

"I have no knowledge of such treatment—"

"That will be determined at the hearing, sir," Fredericks interrupted. "As of now, you are relieved of command of Fort Sill."

Fredericks turned, walked to the door and called Mackenzie's staff sergeant from the outer office.

"Sergeant, I have relieved Colonel Mackenzie of his command. You will inform all of the officers and the men of this. My orders are in the colonel's hand, please feel free to examine them."

"Uh, yes, sir," said the confused sergeant. He crossed the room and took the orders from Mackenzie's limp hands and read them thoroughly.

"Are you satisfied?" Fredericks asked him.

"Yes, sir."

"Good. You will witness that I have relieved the colonel, and you may so inform the men. Dismissed."

"Uh, yes, sir," the sergeant said. He handed Fredericks the orders and left the room.

"Colonel, you will please vacate the premises and return to your home until further notice."

Mackenzie stared at both of us with the fury plain in his eyes.

"You haven't heard the last of this," he said tightly, "both of you. I'll get in touch with Grant myself."

"Please feel free to do so, sir," Fredericks said.

Mackenzie gathered up his gunbelt and hat, removed his saber from the wall, and stomped out of the office, slamming the door behind him.

"Jesus Christ," I said, "what a relief."

"We might as well stay here a while rather than go back to your hotel, Clint," he said, walking around to the other side of the desk. "You can rest a while."

I dropped myself wearily into a chair and said, "Why don't you search that desk for a bottle?"

He did so, and came up with one that was half full of whiskey. We passed it back and forth while I told him what had been going on at Fort Sill for the past week or so.

"I can see where Mackenzie's obsession got the better of him," he said when I was finished. "It's a shame. From what I've heard he was a damned good officer."

"Until Fort Sill, and Quanah."

"And you, I guess."

"I guess I'll take some credit."

"Sergeant Teal was the soldier in the stockade?" he asked.

"Yeah."

"We'll take care of him and the others later on. What about the serial numbers you sent me, for the Colts. Where are the guns?" he asked.

"They're underneath the saloon, which is owned by Jed Jordan."

"The man Quanah said was selling him the guns?"

"Yes."

He shook his head and said, "I find that part of the story incredible. He actually gave you the name of the man who's been supplying him with guns . . . and you believe him?"

"I do. He's a man of honor, Bill."

"Yes, well, Lord knows there're few enough of them around, aren't there?"

Bill Fredericks and I had met when he was a sergeant and I was a deputy U.S. marshall. We worked on a case together involving gunrunning, and had become friends. We had kept in touch on and off for the last ten years, so that I usually knew where he was. This was the first time I'd seen him in two years, and he hadn't changed much. He was a big man, about my age. He had dark hair and had added a mustache since the last time I saw him. He'd made captain a couple of years ago, and was due to move up again soon.

Maybe as a result of this. Breaking Jordan's operation would be a feather in his cap.

"If Jordan's been the one selling Quanah the guns," he said, "and stealing them from army shipments, then he must have been getting inside information."

"Makes sense."

"Do you think Mackenzie could be involved?"

I thought about that a moment, then said, "I doubt it, Bill. Like you said, I think M. kenzie's been a good officer for most of his career. 1 could have let Teal shoot me down out there on the ʒtaked Plains, but he chose to bring me back."

"Yes, but he wasn't above letting them work you over for him," he reminded me.

"I think that was only because of his wife," I said.

"His wife?"

"Uh, yeah. Blonde, very attractive . . ."

"I see," he said, shaking his head at me. I smiled sheepishly, the first time I'd smiled in days. It felt funny, like my face was stretching.

"Okay, then, what about this Sergeant Teal and his crew?" he asked.

"Working with Jordan?" I asked, and he nodded. "Now that's a possibility. They killed a man the night I got away from them."

"So you said. Do you know what became of his body?"

"No idea."

"We'll have to find it. The big man, Dutch Black, I saw him in the infirmary. Couldn't miss a monster like him. What'd you hit him with?"

"My good intentions. What about Clinch?"

"I don't know him by name, but I've seen a corporal walking around with his arm in a sling."

"That's him."

"Just the four of them?"

"Yup."

"What about the rest of the soldiers?"

"Seem to be regular army, from what I could gather."

"That's good. They'll follow orders."

He got up and said, "Okay, let's get you to your hotel and into bed."

"What about Jordan—"

"I'll take care of Jordan, Clint, don't worry. As far as I'm concerned, you're in the clear, and that's what you've been wanting, isn't it?"

"Actually, yes, but I'd still like to—"

I started to get up as I spoke, and I guess it was a combination of fatigue, hunger, and a quarter of a bottle of whiskey on an empty stomach, because I felt myself pitching over and the last thing I heard was Fredericks calling out, "Sergeant!"

Chapter Forty-Five

Fredericks came to see me the next day while I was still in bed and gave me the bad news.

"Gone," he said, "all of them."

"They were there!"

"I believe you, Clint. They were there, but now they're gone. Someone either tipped Jordan off, or he's sold them."

"Not to Quanah," I said.

"Why not?"

"I don't think he'd want them," I started, and went on to explain my theory behind that.

"Well, then, maybe he's hidden them somewhere else."

"What about Teal and the others?"

"They're gone, too."

"Jesus Christ, is Mackenzie still around?"

"He is, but his wife's moved out on him."

"She left town?"

He shook his head and said, "She's here in the hotel. She'd like to know if she can come up and see you."

"Tell her sure. But let me get dressed first."

"Why, you shy? Got something she hasn't seen yet?"

I gave him a dirty look and said, "Get out of here. Find those guns."

"You get a commission or something?" he asked, rising.

"Sorry, captain," I said. "Please find those guns?"

"That's much better," he said, grinning.

"Listen, Bill, can you hold onto command of Fort Sill?"

"No problem," he replied. "My orders are explicit."

"What about Mackenzie? Can he still make trouble for me . . . and you, for that matter?"

"Not if we find those guns," he assured me.

"Well, I'm glad you believe me that I've seen them."

"You didn't make up those serial numbers, Clint. We shipped those guns from Washington by rail, and they disappeared. If they're right here in Fort Sill, I'm going to find them, and then Mackenzie will have all the trouble he can handle and no time to try and make any for someone else."

"Yeah, I guess it's pretty damaging that those guns have been here in Fort Sill all along, but I still don't think he was aware of it."

"Well, it'll all become clear when I find those guns and arrest Jed Jordan. Listen, you get dressed and I'll send Mrs. Mackenzie up."

I threw the covers back and got to my feet, saying, "Go ahead down and send her up. We'll talk again later. How about dinner?"

"Fine," he said, moving towards the door. "I'll see you then."

By the time I was pulling on my boots there was a knock at the door.

"Come in."

The door opened and Sheila Mackenzie came in.

"Oh, you're up and around," she said, looking surprised. "I thought you were badly injured."

"Not badly," I said, "but that doesn't mean that I can't use some sympathy."

I was joking, but she didn't seem to notice. She looked very serious and obviously had something weighing heavily on her mind.

"What's wrong, Sheila?"

"I don't know what to do," she said.

"For a start you can sit down."

She sat down on the bed and let her hands lie limply in her lap.

"What's wrong?" I asked again.

"When Ronald came home yesterday he was ranting and raving about what had happened," she said. "I had to get out of that house, Clint. I was afraid of him. During our marriage, I've felt a lot of things for him, but never fear. I practically ran from the house and came here to get a room."

"Well, you probably did the right thing," I said.

"He hates you, Clint. He blames you for everything that's happened to him."

"I suppose that's because I did have something to do with it, but most of it is his own doing."

"I realize that, but you should be very careful."

"I intend to."

"Good." She got up from the bed to leave, but she was hesitating for some reason.

"Sheila, what else is on your mind?" I asked.

She looked at me as if she were afraid to tell me, then said, "You and me."

"Sheila—"

"I just thought that since we were at the hotel together," she said, rushing on, "we might be able to—"

"You told your husband about us, didn't you?" I asked.

She dropped her eyes and said, "Yes."

"Why?"

"I wanted to hurt him."

"And did you?"

Shaking her head she said, "I don't really know, Clint."

She looked up at me, her blue eyes brimming with tears. I can't stand to see a woman cry, so I took her in my arms and gave her a long, deep kiss. We both threw our backs into it, as if that was the last kiss either one of us would ever get on earth. When it was over, Sheila looked up at me again.

There were no tears in her eyes as she said, "Goodbye, Clint."

I told her goodbye and she was gone.

I was strapping on my gun when a thought hit me. I wondered what they had done with Duke when they brought me back and threw me in a cell. I decided to go and find Bill Fredericks before our dinner meeting.

Chapter Forty-Six

When I was passing through the lobby on my way out, I saw old man Jordan coming out of a door behind the front desk, which seemed to lead to a staircase.

"Hello, Pop," I said.

"Eh?" he said, jerking his head around. He closed the door behind him, then said, "Oh, hello, young fella. You feeling better now?"

"A lot better, Pop, thanks."

He leaned on the desk and said, "I hear you think my boy has been selling guns to the Indians."

"I'm sorry about that, Pop—" I started to apologize, but he cut me off.

"Don't apologize, son," he said. "I wouldn't put something like that past him. If he done it, he deserves whatever he gets, that's what I say."

"I'm sorry, Pop," I said again, for want of something better to say.

I left the hotel and walked over to the fort. It was the first time I had walked into that compound without feeling like a walking target. At the C.O.'s office, the same staff sergeant was sitting behind the desk.

"Is Captain Fredericks in?" I asked him.

"I'm afraid not, Mr. Adams," he answered. All of a sudden I was "Mr." Adams. "I don't know where he is."

195

"Do you know what they did with my horse when they brought me back here the other day?"

"Yeah, he's in our stables, being taken good care of, from what I hear. Most of the men are very impressed with him."

I was used to that.

"I'm going to go over and check on him myself. I hope you're right about his care."

"Don't worry," he said. "When you're in the calvary, you learn to respect horses."

"I hope so. Thanks."

"Sure." He picked up a piece of paper that looked like some kind of a schedule, and on the top I saw the word "Armory". He started to bring it into Mackenzie's— that is, Fredericks's—office.

"What's that?" I asked him.

"This? It's a schedule of shipments from the armory for Captain Fredericks."

"If Colonel Mackenzie was still in command, would he be getting that?"

"Sure. The armory keeps us up on all of their shipments and schedules."

"Okay, thanks."

I walked over to the stables and found Duke in fine shape.

"Hey, you look good, big boy. I guess army life agrees with you, huh?"

I left Duke at the livery stable, which was temporarily being run by a friend of Freddie's.

I spent a little more time trying to locate Fredericks, but when I couldn't I decided that there wasn't anything on my mind that couldn't wait until dinner, now that I knew Duke was all right.

I considered going to the saloon for a drink, but running into Jed Jordan right then might not have been such a good idea, so I decided to go over to the café and have a cup of coffee, instead.

The thing that was uppermost in my mind at the moment was where else Jordan could have hidden those guns, and in order to move them he had to have had some help—from Joe Teal and his friends?

Dutch Black must have come in handy when it came to moving those cartons, but Dutch and Jack Clinch were out of commission, so Jordan must have had to move the stuff with only Teal and Brady to help.

How far could they have moved it? They couldn't have driven a buckboard loaded down with guns out of town without being seen, so those guns still had to be somewhere in town.

But where?

Over a second cup of coffee, I started to get a good idea as to where, and also about how Jordan worked the thefts of the guns, *and* where he might have gotten his information about the shipments.

I finished up my coffee and got up to leave the café. There were a couple of things I wanted to look into before I met Bill Fredericks for dinner.

Chapter Forty-Seven

A couple of hours later, I returned to the café and had only been seated a few moments when Fredericks walked in.

"I heard you were looking for me," he said, sitting down.

"I was, but it wasn't anything important ... . then."

"Meaning?"

"I think I have the answer to our problem."

"Our problem?"

"Our problem," I said again. "I'd like to know where those guns went, too . . . and I think I do."

"Where?"

"I also think I know where Jordan's been getting his information," I went on.

"Are you going to keep me in suspense?" he asked.

"I just want to—"

He held his hand up and said, "Yes, I guess you are. I'm going to order dinner first. This can wait until I order dinner, can't it?"

"We have all night," I said. "My plan won't be put into effect until tomorrow," I explained, and when he arched an eyebrow I hastily added, "That is, if you agree with it."

"Let me order," he said, "and then we'll talk about this plan of yours."

200

We called the waitress over and we both ordered a simple steak and potatoes dinner and a beer. She brought the beer first, and when she left we resumed our conversation.

"All right, so tell me this plan of yours."

I outlined my theory for him step by step, and then did the same with my plan. When I was finished he started to nod, mulling it over.

"I have to admit, it sounds reasonable," he said, "and your plan will probably work."

"What about Dutch Black? Is he out of the infirmary?"

"He's still got a headache that beats any hangover you or I have ever had, but he's on his feet."

"He'll probably know where Teal and the others are."

"And Jordan just stays behind that bar of his, brazen as can be. He practically laughed in our face when we searched his storeroom and came up empty."

"Well, if my plan works, he won't be the one laughing tomorrow night."

He raised his beer and said, "That'll be worth seeing. There's no telling how many deaths he's caused army personnel by selling those guns to Quanah."

"Yes, but he hasn't made it easy for them, either."

"How do you mean?"

"He sold them the guns, but only limited amounts of ammunition," I explained.

"So that they'd have to go back to him for more," he finished. "Say what you want about him, he's probably a very good businessman."

"If he'd only stuck to his business."

During dinner I told Bill why I had originally been looking for him, and he took credit for Duke's good treatment.

"I told them that if that animal lost even one pound, they'd be on K.P. for months."

"I appreciate that, Bill."

"Fine animal like that, he should have been an army horse," he said.

"Not on your life. Duke's a free spirit."

"Like you are now," he said. "Have you given up the law for good, Clint?"

"Not the law, Bill," I answered, "just the job of upholding it. Let the others do that. All I am now is a traveling gunsmith."

"That's what you'd like to be, you mean. Your reputation won't let you, though. I heard that you were in Abilene with Hickok."

"I was, but it's not something I want to talk about," I said shortly.

"Have it your way, pal," he said. "Right now I suggest we get some sleep, so we can put your plan into effect bright and early in the morning."

"Good idea."

He walked with me to the hotel, saying, "I'll be at my office early. Come over whenever you're ready."

"Where are you sleeping? In the hotel?"

He shook his head. "There's a cot in the office that will suit me just fine. Once I've got this all cleared up, they'll send a replacement for me, and a permanent replacement for Mackenzie."

"What happens to Mackenzie?"

"He'll go to Washington, pending an investigation and possible reassignment . . . or discharge."

"It's a shame," I remarked. "He let his obsession with Quanah eat at him, and then when I came along I seemed to push him over the edge."

"What is Quanah like?" he asked, as we stopped in front of the hotel.

I shrugged, and thought a moment.

"A great leader, I think. An honorable man. He felt he had a debt to me, and he rode into the fort with me to pay it, even though he knew it might mean his death."

"A brave man, then."

"That goes with being a great leader."

"What's he after? Why doesn't he accept the peace we'd offered him and his people?"

"You know the answer to that as well as I do, Bill," I said. "Revenge is certainly a motivation."

"Revenge?"

"For his mother, his sister. You know the story behind Quanah. His mother was white, captured by the Comanches. She married the chief, had two sons and a daughter. Quanah is the only one who survived—"

"Yes, I know the story."

"And then there is this peace that you've offered," I said. "It's considerably less than what he and his people are used to."

"He'll have to submit, sooner or later," he said, "or die."

"Exactly," I agreed.

I walked up onto the boardwalk and to the door of the hotel, then turned.

"Submit or die," I repeated. "The decision is an easy one . . . for him."

Chapter Forty-Eight

Early the following morning I went to Fredericks's office and was passed through by the staff sergeant.

"What's his name?" I asked Bill.

"Sergeant Richard Meyers. He's been staff sergeant here for the past eight months."

"How long have you been losing shipments from the armory?" I asked.

"About six months."

I nodded with satisfaction.

"Are you ready to play your part?"

He stood up and straightened his hair.

"I always wanted to be on the stage," he said.

We walked to the door of his office and I opened it and stepped into the outer office.

"Well, now that you know where the guns are, I guess you'll go and collect them," I said to Bill.

"I think I'll wait a day," he responded as planned. "I still want to locate Teal and his buddies. Dutch Black has dropped out of sight, too."

"That's some drop," I said, "a man his size."

"Well, he found a hole deep enough somewhere."

"And now you can bury him in it."

I walked to the front door and said, "Will you let me know how it turns out?"

"I'll send you a telegram," he said.

I looked at Sergeant Meyers and said, "Goodbye, sergeant."

"Uh, goodbye, sir," he replied. His mind was obviously on something else, which was what we had intended all along.

I left the office and went straight to my hotel to check out. In the hall I ran into Sheila Mackenzie.

"Are you leaving?" she asked.

"Yes. There's nothing to keep me here any longer," I replied, and then realized that she might interpret my words in a way I hadn't meant them.

"I had hoped to be able to talk to you again," she said, "but I suppose it's just as well this way."

"Sheila, I want to thank you for helping me the way you did," I said. "I—"

"Don't thank me, Clint," she said, interrupting me. "Let's just say goodbye without thanking each other, okay?"

"All right," I agreed. "Goodbye, Sheila."

She stood in the hall with her head down and I walked away and left her there.

"You checking out, young feller?" Pop asked at the desk.

Since I had all my gear in my hands, it was a pretty decent guess on his part.

"I'm checking out, Pop. I've had enough of Fort Sill to last me a lifetime."

"I can't say as I blame you," he said.

He figured my bill and I paid him and picked up my gear.

"You see that no good son of yours around, Pop, tell him I said to pay you what he owes you."

"Ah," he said, waving a hand, "I forgot all about that. Never see that money again. Good luck to you, young feller."

"Yep, good luck to you, too, Pop," I said, and then I added to myself, you're going to need it. You, your son, and his friends.

Chapter Forty-Nine

"It's getting late," Dill Fredericks whispered into my ear.

"I guess they want to make sure the town is totally asleep," I said, hoping that I was right.

We were sitting in the dark behind Pop Jordan's hotel, Fredericks, myself and about ten soldiers scattered around, waiting for the back door to open. Not the back door to the hotel, but the back door to his dugout basement, the one like his son had in his building.

When I'd seen Pop come out of that door behind the desk, it hadn't registered right away what it meant. Not until I was thinking about it over coffee.

Where could Jed Jordan have hidden those guns? All he had to do one night, he and Teal, and probably Sam Brady, was move those wooden crates from his building a few doors down to his old man's hotel, and hide them there. Who'd know? I certainly wouldn't have even thought of it if I hadn't seen Pop Jordan coming out from that door.

The whole thing about Pop and Jed being on bad terms was an act, so nobody would ever suspect that Jed might be hiding guns underneath his father's hotel. That was better than keeping them under his own building permanently. No, when they threw me in a cell and I started talking to Mackenzie about Jed Jordan being the one who was selling guns, Teal must have gone to Jordan and they decided it was time to move the guns . . . and they were right. They moved them just in time to avoid having them found by Captain Fredericks's search.

"What's that?" Bill said suddenly.

I saw what he was referring to. A ray of light showing through the cracks in the doors.

"They're coming up."

"They must be pretty tired of holding up down there," Fredericks remarked, "especially since adding Dutch Black to the crowd."

"Yeah, he's pretty much of a crowd all by himself, isn't he?" I asked.

"Shhh!"

When the doors swung outward, a shaft of light came shining out, and we heard a voice hiss, "Put out that light, you idiot!"

Immediately, the light was blown out. I had turned my head aside, so that when I looked back I still had my night sight. Jordan, coming out of the well-lit basement, wouldn't be able to see anything but pitch black, as was the case with the others.

Jack Clinch came out behind him, his arm still in a sling, and he was followed by Pop Jordan.

"Let's get going," Jordan called back down the steps.

As we watched, Jordan went back down and came backing out, holding one end of a crate while Sam Brady was lugging the other end. From behind them came big Dutch Black, his face still bandaged, carrying one crate all by himself.

"Those the crates?" Fredericks asked in my ear.

"From what I can see——"

"You've got to be sure, Clint," he interrupted me. "If I'm going to take chances with my men's lives, and those men's lives. If they start shooting—"

"Those are the crates," I said now. Even though my eyes were used to the darkness, it was still kind of hard to see, but from what I could see, I had to say that those were the crates I'd seen under Jed Jordan's saloon.

"Okay, then."

He signaled the three soldiers who were carrying storm lamps, and at the same time they each lit their lamp. Fredericks and I stepped forward, as did the ten soldiers, three holding lamps and the others holding rifles.

"Hold it right there," Frederick shouted.

The three lamps lit the area up fairly well, and now I could see the crates plainly—I'd been right.

Jed Jordan wasted no time. He dropped his end of the crate, which hit the ground with a loud crash. At the same time Jack Clinch used his good hand to go for his gun, but I beat him to it. I fired through the sling, throwing him back against the building. Pop Jordan hit the ground as Dutch Black literally threw his crate towards us.

Fredericks and I scrambled away from the large crate and it fell to the ground and came apart. The new Colts' just lay there among the broken wood.

Dutch seemed to forget that he was wearing a gun and started running towards the armed soldiers. They wasted no time firing at him, and as five or six slugs hit him, he staggered back a few feet and fell through the open door and down the stairs.

Clinch had sagged to the ground against the wall and was holding his good hand to his newly injured shoulder. Pop Jordan was still lying flat on the ground, trying to stay out of the firing line.

Sam Brady had frozen when Jordan dropped his end of the crate, and as a result he was screaming because he hadn't been able to hold the crate alone, and it was now pinning both of his hands to the ground.

As we closed on the variously injured group, I looked around and realized that one was missing.

"Damn, what happened to Jordan?"

Nobody seemed to know. It seemed that everyone had been watching the crate thrown by Dutch Black, and then they'd been watching Dutch himself, waiting for him to make a move.

During the commotion, Jed Jordan had disappeared.

"Where could he have gone?" Fredericks asked.

"Back down the steps," I said, and I started down after him.

I heard Fredericks behind me, ordering his men to round all of the prisoners up, and then I could hear him running down the steps behind me.

I had fogotten about Dutch who was now lying at the foot of the steps, and tripping over his body saved my life.

As I went sprawling to the floor, the room was lit by the muzzle flashes of Jordan's gun as he fired twice. I heard Bill Fredericks cry out, apparently hit.

I managed to hold onto my gun as I fell and from that position I fired in the direction of the muzzle flashes. There was a loud cry and a large thud as Jordan fell against some boxes, knocking them over.

I waited a few moments, and when I heard no movement from his direction, I pushed myself to my feet.

"Bill," I called out, searching for Fredericks in the darkness. "Bill, are you all right?"

"Light a lamp, for Chrissake," he snapped back at me.

I began to feel along the wall, hoping that there would be a lamp hanging on a nail, and found one. I fished out a match and lit the lamp.

Fredericks was sitting on the second step up, with both feet planted firmly on Dutch Black's bloody chest.

Fredericks was leaking some blood, too, but only from his left arm, which didn't seem to be too bad.

Dutch was dead, and his eyes were open and staring in disbelief.

I turned and looked among the fallen boxes until I located Jed Jordan's body. I'd hit him with both shots I'd fired, dead-center in the chest, and he was dead.

By the lamplight we could see the other cartons that no doubt contained new Colt handguns.

"Well," I said, turning to face Bill Fredericks, "I guess I was right, wasn't I?"

"I guess so," he muttered, holding up his bloody arm. "But I wish we hadn't had to go quite this far to prove it."

Chapter Fifty

Sergeant Meyers was the last of the gang to be rounded up, the following morning. He seemed quite surprised to see me walk in with Captain Fredericks, who had his arm in a sling.

"Sir?" he said, not quite sure what else to say.

Two soldiers walked in behind us and Fredericks informed the staff sergeant that he was to go with the two soldiers, who would escort him to join his friends in a nice, comfortable cell.

When I had seen that armory shipment schedule on Meyers's desk, it occurred to me that he had access to all the information Jed Jordan would need to steal the guns. As it turned out, Teal and his friends had gone in with Jordan, and eventually they had talked Meyers into cooperating as well, although all he did was pass on information.

Apparently, Amos Holt was the nervous type, and Jordan had decided that it was time to get rid of him, and making it look like the Indians did it seemed the best way to him.

Mackenzie had been so intent on catching Quanah, that he had never noticed what was going on right under his nose. Once I realized how it was being done, Fredericks and I had put on that little act about giving it one more day before grabbing the guns. We wanted Jordan to think he had that night to move them again. Now his father, Teal, Brady and Clinch were all under arrest, and Dutch Black and Jordan himself were dead.

When Meyers had been led away, Fredericks and I went into his office. He sat down behind his desk and said, "Why don't you pour us a couple of drinks. The bottle is in the desk, and I brought in some glasses, as well."

"Jesus," I said, digging out the bottle, "one little bullet wound and he wants to be waited on."

He glared at me, but didn't reply.

"Here's to success," I said to him, raising my glass and handing him his.

"You call this success?" he asked, indicating his wounded arm.

"Well, I'm in the clear, all the guilty parties are accounted for, and you got your nice shiny new Colts back."

"And Quanah is still out there with a load of Winchester Seventy-threes, waiting to pick off my soldiers."

"Your soldiers?"

"Well, they're mine until I'm replaced."

"Okay, so Quanah's got rifles, but he doesn't have all that much ammunition, remember?" I reminded him. "And what happens when he runs out of ammunition? What's he got then?"

He smiled and said, "Empty rifles, useless empty rifles. You're right, let's drink to success."

"Of course, they're only empty until he can find someone else to supply him with ammo," I pointed out.

He glared at me again and this time said, "Don't you know when to leave well enough alone?"

"Sure I do," I said. I put down my whiskey, got up and walked to the door. "Right now. Goodbye, Bill. I'll keep in touch."

"Clint," he called before I could walk out.

"What?"

"Thanks," he said, and then indicating his arm again, he added, "For most of it."

I gave him a casual salute and left his office.

Outside I climbed up onto my wagon—from which, miraculously, nothing was missing—and drove out the front gates of Fort Sill, with Duke trailing along behind.

As I drove my team through that maze of teepees, I thought again about Dancing Willow, Dancing Fawn and, most of all, Quanah.

His supply of guns was gone, dried up—at least temporarily. But he had been perfectly willing to give it up anyway, in order to pay his debt to me. He knew, as well as Fredericks and I did, that sooner or later someone else would come along, looking to make a few dollars at the cost of a few hundred, or thousand lives, red and white.

How much time did Quanah have, though, I wondered? How much time before enough soldiers were sent after his people. How many of his people would die before he finally submitted . . . or died himself?